THE ASSASSIN'S VENGEANCE

JASON DRAKE BOOK 3

AUSTON KING

FOREWORD

To sign up for my mailing list, please visit: www.creatorcontact.com/ auston-king/
The mailing list will be only be used to update you about upcoming releases. Nothing more.

Thank you for purchasing this book. A lot of time and effort has gone into it and I truly hope you enjoy it.

If you spot any errors, typos with this copy, or would just like to say hi, please let me know by emailing: austonking@creatorcontact.com

I am always interested in hearing what people think about my work.

Thank you,
Auston King

PROLOGUE

A modified Mil Mi-8 helicopter flew over southern Ukraine. It was just past midnight and rainy. The twin-turbine helicopter sped through the dark at about half its service ceiling—16,000 feet—partially because of the bad weather, partially because it was close to the AO. The pilot glided the bird along the shoreline. The Black Sea's waters loomed out to the edge of the horizon and vanished into dark nothingness.

Flying at a speed of 190 knots, the helicopter could barely be heard by those in the houses that sporadically dotted the coastline. The additional blades that had been attached to its rotor system helped minimize its sound. It was the same technology used by the modified Sikorsky UH-60 Black Hawk helicopter, which helped US Navy SEAL Team 6 take out Osama Bin Laden in his Pakistan shelter. The only reason the world had known about the modified Black Hawk's technology was because SEAL Team 6 had to trash it during the operation. If not for one simple mishap, the world would not have known a thing.

Those inside the Mi-8 were Ukrainian special forces. There were six of them in total, and they were ready for anything. Rain pelted their faces from the half-opened side door of the helicopter.

The squad lead's codename was 'Bear.' His face felt numb from the cold and wind. He had a long scar that stretched from his upper right cheek to his lower left jaw. The men in his unit believed it'd been given to him by a bear, hence the codename. But Bear never told them the truth about where the scar came from or how he earned the codename.

The five members of his squad were quiet. They were all strapped to the inside chassis of the helicopter. Their eyes narrow, their breathing slow. The only thing that mattered to them was the mission. Like Bear, they all had battle scars. Some were etched on their bodies; some were of the more psychological variety.

Every soldier has a scar.

Bear checked his watch, looked out the window, and then performed one final equipment check. He examined his tactical vest, kevlar armored body shield, and assault rifle.

His weapon of choice was the Fort-221, a specially modified version of the CTAR-21 made by Israel Military Industries. It was a bullpup assault rifle, which meant the action was behind the trigger instead of in front of it. It made the weapon lighter and more compact. It was an ideal weapon of choice for a mission like this. Attached to Bear's weapon were a holographic sight and under-barrel bipod.

Satisfied with his equipment check, Bear tapped the man on his right to get his attention.

The young squad member looked at his squad leader and nodded.

They were ready.

The helicopter pulled away from the shoreline and sped two klicks north toward a small, open field. It was a location far enough away from anyone on the ground as not to arouse suspicion.

This mission required them to be invisible. If they burst into the AO guns-a-blazing, they'd risk a lot—potentially a war with Russia. Maybe even a world war.

Still, the mission was simple: capture the smuggler and bring him in for questioning.

Yet, completing the mission was going to be difficult.

No mission is easy.

Ukrainian intelligence had received word that an anti-Russian rebel group was about to pick up a shipment of chemical weapons from a smuggler at Ochakiv Port. The smuggler was delivering the weapons from Turkey.

Ukrainian intelligence believed the rebels were planning to use the chemical weapons on Russian forces stationed in Crimea—a retaliation of sorts for the Russian Army's recent aggression and military build-up in the region.

A part of Bear empathized with the rebels' aim. They were men who wanted to take back their land. The Russians had invaded the Crimean Peninsula just a decade earlier, and the recent build-up of Russian Army forces along the Ukrainian border was more than unsettling.

The problem was the rebels' actions could incite, and perhaps even justify, a Russian military invasion. If Ukraine couldn't stop its own people, the Russians would.

The Russian military would make mincemeat of the rebels. And, if Bear knew anything about Russia, it was that they'd make sure that any rebel organization in Ukraine would think twice before attacking them again. Their message would be loud and bloody and involve the lives of Ukrainian civilians.

Bear and his men needed to stop the rebels from inflaming the Russian military's aggression. He'd have to stop the anti-Russian rebels from killing Russian soldiers.

He thought it was a funny assignment when he first heard it. Ironic, almost.

"You want me to protect the lives of Russian soldiers? Do you know how many I've killed?"

His commanding officer nodded. He was a short man with a wrinkly face and long, stringy eyebrows. "The Russians are just waiting for us to blink," the officer said. "They've accused us of not being able to take care of our own. The build-up of their forces along our eastern border has our president worried. You need to stop those rebels before they accidentally start a war. This isn't about those soldiers you're saving. It's about the lives you'll save from a potential war."

Bear accepted the mission.

The rebels collecting the weapons were a ragtag group. They were all untrained, and before the conflict with Russia had picked up, they were farmers or fishermen. They weren't soldiers.

"We need to find out how the hell a group of underpaid misfits afforded a shipment of chemical weapons," his commanding officer said. "Get that smuggler. Bring him in. Alive."

"Of course," Bear said.

The helicopter glided down to the ground. The tall grass around the bird swirled in a violent fashion. Once the landing pads hit the damp grass, Bear and the rest of his team jumped out and hid within the grass's density.

"Follow me!" Bear grunted.

The commandos followed Bear toward the shore—toward Ochakiv Port.

Behind them, the helicopter pilot turned off the bird's engine and brought its rotors to a standstill.

Bear and the commandos maneuvered through a small forest. They moved like shadows, staying in lockstep with each other. The smells of the early morning soil filled their nostrils. The sounds of birds chirping in the trees echoed among the trees. A light fog rose from the damp earth.

"Ochakiv Port is up here," Bear said, loud enough that the others could all hear, but not so loud to give away his position to any cautious ears. "Just over this ridge. Are you ready?"

His men nodded.

They climbed to the top of the ridge and looked down a small incline. One hundred yards from their position was the port.

The port was small and nondescript. Four large storage buildings, built from corrugated steel, loomed along the water's edge. It was used by local fishermen—no one else. The boats that docked at its wooden piers were mostly small and old. One boat stood out beside the pier, however. A small panga skiff with a raised bow.

Bear pulled out a pair of night-vision goggles from his backpack and scanned the area.

The AO was busy. There were at least twenty men on the jetties.

They were armed, holding AK-47s and shotguns. Those not patrolling the dock were moving small, wooden crates from the panga skiff. A group of rebels were drinking vodka—a premature celebration.

"Let's break up the party," Bear muttered to his men. "These assholes don't know what they're risking. Come on."

The six commandos made their way down the grassy incline toward Ochakiv.

Once at a small, rusted chainlink fence that surrounded the eastern edge of the storage buildings, Bear lifted his right arm, signaling his men to stop their advance. He and his men knelt down and hid within the shadow cast by one of the buildings.

Two of his men pulled out some cutters and created a small hole in the fence.

Bear followed his men inside.

Hugging the corrugated steel wall of the building, they moved toward the edge of the dock. At the corner of the building, Bear moved to the lead.

He turned back to his men and motioned with his hands that a target was coming close.

A drunk rebel stumbled toward the shadows where Bear and his men hid. The poor bastard was oblivious. He had a bottle of vodka in one hand, and he was trying to unbuckle his pants with the other.

"I'll get him," Bear whispered to his men.

He kept his rifle slung around his shoulder and waited for the rebel to pass.

The rebel stumbled to the dock's edge, giggling. He tossed back the final few sips of vodka from the bottle and then threw it into the ocean.

Crouching, Bear moved toward the rebel, grabbing him by the neck. He rendered the drunk asshole unconscious. He held the body and dragged it back to the shadows where his men hid.

"Let's go," Bear said. "Stay silent and drop them all before the smuggler can get away. We need him alive. We'll meet on the dock."

His men nodded and split up. Two followed Bear, and three

went in the other direction. The strategy was to take on the rebels from both sides.

Bear lifted his rifle and held it snugly at his shoulder. He and the two squad mates with him moved around the corner of the building.

The rebels didn't have a chance. The shots from the commandos came from all directions. They didn't realize what was going on. They panicked. When they did figure it out, they either tried in vain to fight back or fled—climbing the fence that surrounded the dock or jumping into the cold water. Those who fought back died. Those who fled, Bear didn't care about.

During the action, the smuggler on the small skiff began to untie his boat from the pier. He'd just turned the engine on when Bear and his men got onto the deck of the boat.

"Stand down," Bear shouted at the smuggler.

The smuggler raised his arms. He was smart enough to know there was no point in trying to run.

Bear and his men grabbed hold of the smuggler. They put a bag over his head and handcuffed his wrists. They pulled him off the boat and escorted him back to the helicopter.

The three other commandos who'd separated from Bear before the shooting began secured the port and took images of the boat and pictures of the containers that were being unloaded. They'd wait there for a squad of Ukrainian military soldiers to arrive.

Fifteen minutes after the shooting had started, Bear, his men, and the smuggler arrived back at the field where the helicopter waited. They placed the smuggler into the hull. They cuffed him to a seat and strapped themselves in as it took off into the dark.

The clouds began to break, and the moon's light cut through the sky. Bear smiled. The ride back to base would be pleasant.

Everything had gone to plan.

He called his commander in Kyiv. "The mission is complete," he said. "The chemical weapons are secured, and the rebels are either dead or on the run. We have the smuggler. We're bringing him in."

"Good," the commander said. "You boys have just stopped a war."

The helicopter sped off into the milky, foggy light.

Bear opened a flap on his combat vest and pulled out a cigar. He lit it up and stared at the smuggler, the man with the bag on his head.

"They're going to make you talk," he said. "I know where they're taking you. Temny Facility. Everyone who ends up in Temny talks."

Bear smiled, exhaled a thick plume of smoke, and watched the dark of the sea disappear.

PART 1 - THE SMUGGLER

ONE

Ex-CIA operative Jason Drake walked through the market pathway in the tiny Thai village, Sansor. The village was located ten miles south of Phuket and was popular among tourists. He'd spent the last six months there, having rented a beach cabin that overlooked the Andaman Sea. The rental cost him less than ten US dollars per night. It was cheap, even for Thailand, but that was why he chose it.

He needed a place where he could blend in and lie low.

If he was going to go home, he needed to hide in a place full of vermin.

The overbearing Thai humidity made his clothes stick to his skin. He held a small package in his arms and looked back at the post office where he'd picked it up with a grimace on his face.

Were they catching on? he thought. Were they beginning to ask questions they shouldn't ask? Would he have to run? Again.

He was dressed in a partially buttoned-up blue and red shirt and brown khaki pants that were rolled up slightly at the ankles. He wore dock shoes, a Dallas Stars ball cap, and had a thick five o'clock shadow. He looked like any other tourist in the area—which, of course, was the point.

The market pathway was bustling. Packed to the brim with tourists seeking adventure, pleasure, or something illegal.

The vermin of Sansor were out in full force.

Tiny huts made of bamboo and palm tree were on either side of the path. Each hut sold trinkets, all of them advertised as being handcrafted or genuine. The truth behind each of the beautifully carved wooden Buddhas and dragons that adorned the shelves inside was that they were all made on an assembly line in Bangkok. They were about as authentic as a reality television show about love.

The pathway from the village to the beach was jam-packed. Gullible tourists cluttered the narrow street to the point that it was starting to annoy Drake. He wanted to get back to his cabin. He needed to find out if she had pulled through.

He was about to push past a plump tourist, who had his wallet sticking out of the back of his shorts, when he spotted a young thief sneak up behind him. The thief had his eyes on the man's wallet.

Drake grunted.

The young thief was smooth, quick with his hands. He snatched the wallet from the back pocket without the tourist noticing a thing and hopped through the crowd, disappearing like a shadow in the dark.

The tourist didn't notice his wallet was gone. He wouldn't notice until he went to pay for the underage girl he was escorting around the village. The asshole was one of those sick individuals who'd come to Thailand for the wrong reasons.

Drake scanned the market, looking for the nearest spot where the young thief could have disappeared.

He found it. A small alleyway between two huts. Only the soberest of tourists would have noticed it.

His suspicions were confirmed when he saw the thief's footprints in the mud outside the alley's entrance. The kid was getting sloppy. If he kept pickpocketing tourists like that, he'd end up in a Thai prison.

Drake pushed past the two huts and walked down the narrow alley, making sure his steps were light and quiet.

He found the kid sitting on a bamboo basket at the far end of the alley. The alley led to a dead end. There was nowhere for the kid to run.

The kid was rummaging through the wallet, tossing anything that didn't matter into the mud. He was unaware of Drake.

Drake cleared his throat.

The kid looked up and made an ugly face. "Ah, not you! Ah, this is bullshit, man!"

The young thief spoke English well. He was smart. His name was Pok Dam Sat. English was his fourth language. He also knew French, English, and bits of German. He'd grown up on the streets of Phuket, surviving by any means necessary.

"How much did you score?" Drake asked.

"A couple of thousand baht, not much. These assholes don't carry cash like they used to. The pimps around here have started to accept credit cards."

The kid tossed the wallet onto the ground in front of Drake in frustration.

"It's because of kids like you," Drake said. "The pimps can't have their clientele broke when they go to pay. You've incentivized them to find another means of transaction."

"It's bullshit."

"It's the truth, kid. You don't have to like it."

Pok stuffed the paper bills he'd pulled from the wallet into his pocket. "Did you see his ID? He's some computer engineer from Seattle. He's come here to prey on young girls. You really want to defend guys like that?"

Drake knelt down and picked up the tourist's identification. He examined the photo on the company ID card. The tourist worked for a big software company—one of the largest in the world. Drake put the wallet in his back pocket.

"There are bad men everywhere," Drake said. "Get used to it."

"What are you going to do?"

"I'll find him and give him his wallet back."

"You're not going to teach him a lesson?"

"He's an idiot. He'll make a mistake. Either a pimp will kill him, rob him—or he'll end up caught by the police."

"Most of the police around here pretend this kind of stuff doesn't happen."

"Well, that's the way the world works, kid."

"I thought you were a good guy."

"I'm not."

"You're better than most of the tourists who come around here. You treat the locals with respect. You don't take advantage of our women."

"Hate to break it to you, but I'm one of the bad guys."

"I don't believe you."

"Listen," Drake said. "I came here to tell you that if you keep stealing from these assholes in broad daylight, you're going to be the one who pays. You need to move in the dark, like I told you. That's when you should be pickpocketing. The next time you do this, you'll end up in the back of a police car."

"But there's more targets out in the day."

"Beggars can't be choosers."

Pok shrugged, stood up, and dusted off his pants. "I don't get you," he said to Drake.

"You don't need to."

The two of them walked back down the alley toward the hustling street.

"What's in the package?" Pok asked, noticing what Drake was holding.

"Nothing."

Drake looked left and right down the street. He was looking for the tourist. It didn't take long for him to spot him. The tourist hadn't gone far. He was about to walk up to the tourist and hand back his wallet when he noticed something that he couldn't shake.

The girl beside the tourist. Her eyes were glazed. Her wrists were scarred. Whoever gave her to the plump man from Seattle kept her drugged up.

Could he just let this happen?

He clenched his jaw and tried to come up with an excuse to not help. After all, he was a killer. One trained by the CIA to murder political or military targets. He wasn't a good man.

The young girl fell to her knees. She was so drugged, she could barely stand. The tourist struggled to lift her up.

"Come on, come on!" the man from Seattle said. "I paid good money for you. You can pass out in the hotel. We're almost there. I want to get something for my kid first."

Drake closed his eyes and took a long, deep breath. He then looked back at Pok. The young thief was still at the entrance of the alley. The kid had a broken look on his face, like someone he looked up to had failed him.

Drake knew the feeling well. "Damnit," he grunted to himself.

He walked back to Pok, the tourist's wallet still in his pocket.

"You didn't give him the wallet," Pok said.

"No."

"Why?"

"We're going to wait right here and follow him."

"What?" Pok had a confused look on his face. "Why?"

Drake lifted his index finger and signaled to Pok to stay quiet. They waited at the edge of the dense crowd for the tourist to continue his trek down the market. Drake was going to show Pok how to take care of men like the computer engineer.

TWO

In the center of Moscow was the Kremlin, the fortified complex that was formerly the Tsar's Moscow residence but now served as the chief residence for the Russian President. In Russian, the word *kremlin* meant 'fortress inside a city.' That definition was fitting. It was a fortress.

It was surrounded by a unique triangular wall that varied in thickness, ranging at points between eleven to twenty-one feet. The area within the triangular wall measured at about 2.9 million square feet and housed a variety of buildings, many of which were the most important in Russia. One of those buildings was The Grand Kremlin Palace.

In the study on the top floor of The Grand Kremlin Palace sat President Sergei Makarov and his top general, Yuri Ulanov. The two men faced each other, separated only by a small, wooden table, atop which was an immaculate chess set.

They were in the middle of an intense game. They played in front of a large window that overlooked the Moskva River, which cut through Moscow like a deep scar.

Rain pattered against the window, leaving globular patterns that distorted the gardens below, making the world outside seem like a scene from an impressionist painting. The workers and military officers who walked about the premises seemed to blend into their drab surroundings. They seemed almost to be a part of the very things they were protecting.

The Russian President wasn't focused on the world outside the palace, though. Not at that moment, at least. He knew how drab and dire it was outside.

He felt he understood Russia better than anyone. He'd grown up in a poor family in Leningrad. His father was a cook, and his mother was a factory worker. They both were dead by his twelfth birthday. If not for his good grades, he would have ended up on the streets. It was because of those grades that he'd been invited to be a member of the Soviet Union's Vladimir Lenin All-Union Youth Pioneer organization when he was thirteen. The goal of the organization was to instill in its pupils the importance of social co-operation. Ultimately, the organization's goal was indoctrination.

Makarov stood out at school for his quickness at picking up languages and his physical prowess—he'd become obsessed with sambo and judo, which he practiced for hours on end. He was as adept at the martial arts as he was at French and English.

Attending the Youth Pioneer's school led him to make connections with important people. One of those connections helped him get a job in the KGB. It was just before the fall of the Berlin Wall in 1989.

At first, he worked as a press clippings collector. That job had him read through international news stories. He'd clip the stories out of the papers and send them to the appropriate department for analysis or documentation.

Like all other things in his life, he excelled at his job.

Thanks to the recommendation of his KGB commanding officer, he was selected to train within the elite espionage Andropov Red Banner Institute.

Russia during this time was within the midst of great change. Communism to Democracy. Some said it was death to life. In Russia, the common joke was that it was death to a little less death.

Makarov quickly rose through the ranks of the KGB, which

changed its acronym to SVR. The men in power wanted to dissolve the stain of communist Russia's past.

After years at the SVR, Makarov found himself selected to be an advisor on international affairs for President Boris Yeltsin.

He climbed up the government ladder.

When Yeltsin resigned, Makarov seized the advantage.

It was all just a game. A chess match. That was how he saw all of life.

After Yeltsin resigned, Makarov took power and found himself the head of state of one of the most powerful militaries in the world. With over 6,400 nuclear warheads at his disposal, Makarov knew he had power.

But he wasn't done playing. He wasn't even close.

His brow furrowed, and he stroked his chin. He sat on an old wooden chair painted gold with thick, red velvet cushions.

"It's your move, Mr. President," General Ulanov said.

The study in the palace had a unique smell to it. Thick bookcases lined its walls—tomes full of Russian poetry, strategy, and history. Words and pages written during the time of the great Russian empires of the past.

"You must wait," Makarov said to the general, not lifting his eyes from the board. "I like to ruminate."

"Of course."

Makarov stared at the pieces with fierce intensity. Every move he made was made with purpose.

"While I wait for you to move, I'll do what I came to do," Ulanov said. "I have an update from Ukraine. Our SVR intelligence officers intercepted some intel from their military. Their special forces stopped a shipment of chemical weapons from being delivered to Crimean rebels—anti-Russian. According to the transcript, they believed those weapons were intended to be used on Russian forces stationed on the Crimean Peninsula."

Makarov moved his eyes from the board and looked at Ulanov. "Those rebels have been attacking our soldiers quite a bit lately. It was getting on my nerves," he said.

"Yes," Ulanov said. "And if those rebels hadn't been stopped, I shudder to think how many men we would have lost—hundreds, I think. After the threat you gave the Ukrainian President last week, we'd be in a tight position. We'd have no choice but to go to war."

Makarov nodded. "That's true. I did tell the Ukrainian President that if there was one more attack, we would invade."

"The war would be messy," Ulanov said. "But as long as the Americans don't get involved, we might win. It's shocking that they haven't responded to our build-up at the border."

"War is always messy."

"In any case, it's a good thing the Ukrainians stopped the rebels from securing the weapons," Ulanov said. "The intercept also mentioned that the man smuggling the weapons was captured. They took him to Temny."

Makarov shifted in his seat. He looked away from the board. His focus was elsewhere, but only briefly. Something about Ulanov's words upset him. "Did they get *this* smuggler to talk?"

"That's all the intercept said."

Makarov cracked his knuckles. "Well then," he said. "Let's get back to the game. You've updated me about the latest intel. You did what you came here to do. Thank you."

The President picked up his queen and moved it to a vulnerable spot on the board.

Ulanov's eyes widened. She was clean for the taking. He'd played the President numerous times. Makarov rarely made aggressive moves.

"Make your move," the President said. His voice was low and almost growling.

Ulanov took the President's queen with his rook.

It went back and forth.

Ulanov played like he was going to win. The pieces were falling in his favor.

Makarov was on the defensive.

But Makarov wasn't really on the defensive.

"This game will be over soon," the Russian President said.

Ulanov raised an eyebrow. "With all due respect, Mr. President.

That seems foolish. I own the board. My knight and rook are holding your pieces at bay. From my end, I've won."

Makarov couldn't hide his smile. "It's true. You do appear to have the advantage. You appear to be in control of the situation. You're taking care of things."

"Appear? I will win this game in ten moves."

"I will win it in seven."

Ulanov laughed and shook his head.

Makarov was correct, however. He'd already played it all out in his head. He knew he was going to win.

That was why he liked chess. It was rational, predictable. There was a push and pull to it.

Ulanov took his turn. Makarov took his. After three more moves, Ulanov realized he'd been lulled into a trap. He shook his head. In hindsight, the President's moves looked evident. Makarov had brought back his queen with a pawn. It didn't take him long to snipe off Yuri's queen and rook with the newly resuscitated assassin.

Seven moves later, the game was over.

Makarov won.

"You sacrificed your queen," Ulanov said, dismayed. "Did you mean to do that? Was that your plan all along?"

"The Queen's Gambit. I gave up an essential piece to win the game. Sacrifice."

Ulanov exhaled a deep and heavy breath. "Good game," he said. He stood up.

The two men shook hands. Ulanov left the study.

Makarov walked to his desk and picked up his phone. He called a number.

When he heard the voice on the other end, he breathed a sigh of relief.

"Don't worry," the voice said. "We are taking care of it."

THREE

President Roy Clarkson slammed the paper he was reading down on his desk and walked toward an open window of the oval office. His approach was slowed by the cane he'd been using for the last six months. His steps were labored, off-balance. Once at the window, he realized the effort hadn't been worth it. The warm, humid breeze that brushed against his skin did little to alleviate his unease.

The thick August humidity that settled over the capital that time of year usually made Clarkson feel good, but today was different. He couldn't even enjoy the view. He just festered and brewed.

"I took a damn bullet for this country," he said aloud to himself. His cane shook in his hand. "And this is the respect I get?"

He looked out at the rose garden—the one his wife had spent the last several months remodeling.

"Those damn assholes. No one knows what the hell is going on! If only they knew. This whole damn system is rotten."

Clarkson campaigned for President as an outsider—a man with good business acumen and strong instinct. He'd been a property developer in New York City in the eighties and nineties, and only ran for President after his wife told him he had to. She said that the country needed someone who wasn't beholden to corporate interests, someone with pockets deep enough to fund his own campaign without the need to take what were essentially bribes from the lobbyists that skulked about Constitution Avenue like a plague of rats.

He won. And he did his best to implement what he'd promised, but his business sense was no match for the leeches that inhabited the capital.

He turned away from the garden and hobbled back to his desk. He winced as he sat down and closed his eyes. He took a long, deep breath. The pain emanating through his body had rescinded only briefly.

He didn't look at all like the man the country had elected. Gone was the youthful charm of his first term—his thick brown hair and his healthy complexion were taken with the bullet.

The bullet he'd taken in the neck from a sniper during his second term inauguration.

The Inauguration Day Attack, as the press called it, almost left him paralyzed. The sniper's bullet had taken a chunk of his neck and done serious nerve damage along his spine. Some close to him argued that it took far more.

The attack occurred just as he was about to give his speech on the steps of the Capitol building. He knew he was lucky to survive. Four others were killed by the shooter that day: two were senators, one was his National Security Advisor, and one was a colleague's wife.

Those responsible for the attack were ex-CIA officers. They'd gone rogue and were on a mission of revenge and destruction. They'd been trained by the very country they hated. They wanted blood and chaos.

Thankfully, they had been killed.

But the damage had been done.

Clarkson spent the first three months of his second term in rehab. He recovered. But the press were almost as merciless as the sniper that almost killed him.

"A warmonger," he muttered, rubbing his brow. "They have the damn audacity to call me a *warmonger*. If only they knew."

The journalist who wrote the article was a Harvard-educated twat with tiny wrists and a squeaky voice. He was well-known to Clarkson.

The article accused Clarkson of stoking the flames of war. The journalist concluded that the President wasn't doing enough to avoid a conflict with Russia. The Russians were building up forces along the eastern border of Ukraine. The journalist called the President 'doomed to repeat the mistakes of the past.' He urged the President not to respond to Russia's aggression.

Thinking about the article made Clarkson's blood boil. Every sentence was manufactured to smear his legacy. There wasn't an ounce of truth within it.

The entire article was built upon the words of CIA Director Kate Price. The journalist used her and Clarkson's relationship as the launching off point of his diatribe. When asked about the situation in Ukraine, Price said that the only reasonable response would be to match Russia's build-up.

'Does Clarkson want another Cold War?'

The article concluded with this rhetorical question.

Not once in his many years as President had he tried aggression with Russia. In fact, he was pretty sure the press had accused him of being too soft on Russia after he'd taken office. It disgusted him how fickle the whole system was. No one seemed to have a memory longer than a few seconds. Nothing seemed to matter.

The door to his office opened. It was his secretary. "They're here, Mr. President," she said.

Clarkson nodded. "Send them in."

His secretary left, and three members of the National Security Council entered the room. They were his National Security Advisor Eli Chambers, Director of National Intelligence Steven Gard, and—the focus of the article—CIA Director Kate Price.

It was an emergency meeting called by Clarkson to discuss the article.

The President waited for them to all sit before he began.

"Why do you think I called you in, Kate?" he asked.

Price saw the paper on the desk. "That journalist is an idiot."

"I know," Clarkson said. "But he's an idiot with pull. I'm worried about my legacy. I can't have them frame me as a warmonger. That's not what I am. You need to keep your mouth shut."

"Who cares what they say? You know what you are."

"I care."

Chambers and Gard looked at each other and smiled. They knew why they had been brought in. They were the President's back-up in case Price got feisty. The CIA Director had a reputation for being stubborn and reckless.

Price shifted in her seat. "I just spoke with the Chairman of the Joint Chiefs. We can get a military presence—"

"Enough!" Clarkson snapped. "I'm not sending in our troops."

Stubbornly, Price ignored him. "Based off our latest satellite imagery, Russia is amassing a massive build-up of troops along the eastern border of Ukraine. President Makarov is going to invade—I know it. He's testing us. He's testing our resolve. We need to be there for our allies if they need us. Many of our NATO allies are asking for us to respond to this—"

Clarkson rolled his eyes as Price spoke. "We cannot and should not respond," he said. "With all due respect, Kate, we need to focus on America and America only. Russian military aggression on the Ukrainian border has nothing to do with us. Russia is simply responding to those Crimean rebels that have been causing havoc in the region."

"If we don't respond, Russia will make a mockery of us," she said. "Our allies are worried. They worry an invasion is imminent. If Russia invades Ukraine, where will they stop? If we back down now, it will create chaos—it could destabilize all of Europe."

Clarkson waved his hand in the air dismissively. "The papers are calling me a warmonger," he said. "I don't want to send our soldiers into a conflict I'm not fully committed to winning. No one wants a conflict with Russia. Our country has been through enough lately. We have to be careful."

"That is the right course of action," Chambers said.

"Kiss-ass," Price muttered under her breath.

The Director of National Intelligence chuckled. Gard looked at the President and spoke in an earnest and straightforward way. "With all seriousness, Mr. President, the last thing Russia will do is invade Ukraine. Their generals have assured our military that they won't. The troop build-up is, as Eli said it was, simply meant to dissuade Crimean rebels from attacking their men. We'd do the same thing if Mexican drug lords were attacking cities on our side of the border. You know that."

"Since when are we trusting Russian generals," Price snapped. "Do any of you actually hear yourselves? Russia began that build-up before the attacks on their men started. It was not in response."

"I've had enough, Kate," Clarkson said. "I get it. You think that Makarov wants to invade. And that may be true, but you need to realize I can't risk any kind of international failure. Not now. My second term has just begun. I'd like to leave office with some of my reputation intact. And to be honest, I wouldn't be able to live with myself if I committed our country to another long and drawn-out war. We need to find an alternative solution. I'm surprised you, of all people, don't see that."

"You have a reputation for being overly aggressive, Madam Director," Chambers said to Price, his voice dripping with condescension. "Your Terminus Division, that special group of spies you trained, they turned on us—they shot the President during his inauguration. Your foolhardiness has already cost us so much. Don't let it cost us any more American lives."

"Yes," Gard added. "You should be the last person we listen to right now. How you are still Director of the CIA escapes me."

Price knew both Eli and Gard viewed her as an obstacle and a threat. She ignored their personal attacks and turned to Clarkson. She spoke to him directly. It was her final chance. She knew it. "I don't need to talk about my past. I'm sorry you were shot by former CIA officers... it was awful. But I have never lied to you, Mr. President. I'm not lying right now. We need to take this Russian threat seriously. If we give Russia an inch, they'll take a mile. If we give them Ukraine, Europe will be next. It will be the Cold War all over again—maybe worse. President Makarov isn't like the Soviet leaders of the past. He knows when to be aggressive. He knows we're vulnerable."

Eli and Gard scoffed.

Clarkson looked at his cane. The tool that gave him balance. He sighed. "I'm tired of this," he said. "All I want is this damn country to keep itself together for another three years. That's it. Once I'm out of office, you can get back to your bickering. You all seem to enjoy it so much."

"Sir—"Price said.

"No!" Clarkson shouted, slamming his fist on the desk. "I am a broken man, Kate. I've given this country everything, and it's ruined me. I want out. If peace is an option, we should take it."

"But it won't be—"

"You're simply too much! I've had it. If you want war ... then ..."

"Then what?" she said. It was a challenge. She knew what the President was insinuating. She was ready for it.

Clarkson cleared his throat. "Eli and Steven, you can leave. I want to speak to Kate alone."

The two men straightened their suits as they stood up and left the office. They smirked at Price as they passed her.

"Roy," Price said in a more calm tone, once she was positive Gard and Chambers were gone. "I'm sorry. You know how I am when I get going. I didn't mean to suggest anything. I am ... I don't want war. You know that. All I want is for us to do what's right for our country."

"I am relieving you of your position."

The air was knocked out of Price's lungs. She felt like she couldn't breathe. "Excuse me?"

"I need to be careful, Kate. I have a reputation. You were quoted in the papers suggesting that a troop build-up might be our only option out of this."

"Mr. President, sir, I don't care about your reputation. You know that. I don't care about mine. But if you fire me, you will have no allies left in DC."

"If this was the real estate world, you'd be my most trusted ally. But it's politics," Clarkson said. "I believe you are telling me the truth, but ... I can't."

"Eli and Gard are idiots. They're fools. You need—"

"I'm relieving you of your position, Kate. I'll announce it publicly in a week. If I sided with you right now, the papers—they'd destroy me."

"Screw the papers! This is about national security. You're acting like a fool!"

"I'm in over my head," he said. "I want to do so much for this country, but I can't if you keep talking."

Price looked around the oval office. She wondered if it would be the last time she'd see it. Clarkson had been classy about its presentation—blue curtains, suitable portraits on the walls. Even the desk wasn't ostentatious—it was oak, nothing expensive, but not cheap. There wasn't much a President could decide in the decoration of the White House, but the oval office was one of the few areas where he could make some decisions, where his personality could shine. When she first met him, Clarkson seemed like the real deal, the genuine article.

Seeing him now, she realized just how far he'd fallen.

"You're a fool," she said.

Clarkson took a deep breath. "Easy now," he said.

Price bit her lower lip. "You kick me out right now, and this will come back to haunt you. I swear it will. I've never lied to you. Maybe that was my mistake. Maybe I should have lied more. Like you, I'm not good at these political games. I just want results."

"Yet you lie to yourself, Kate. You're not the saint you think you are. The men who took a chunk of my neck—who tried to kill me—they were your men. You recruited them, trained them. You told me what they did, what their purpose was. I couldn't believe it. I thought that stuff only happened in the movies. A group of killers? Mercenaries who acted outside the law backed by the US government? You act all high and mighty, but you're a fool, too."

"Maybe," she said.

"There's nothing more to discuss," Clarkson said. "I thank you for your service. I need to move on with my life. I need to make sure I have a life after this post. You know what a bad reputation can do to you these days. You have one week to clear things up in the agency. I'd appreciate it if you sent me a list of eligible candidates who could act as director on an interim basis."

"Will do," she said, barely opening her mouth. She seethed. She could hardly even look at Clarkson.

"Very good," Clarkson said. "You can leave."

Price stood up and left the oval office. She didn't look back.

Clarkson picked up the paper and read through the article again. It made him angry, yet it reminded him why he'd just fired his most trusted ally.

He was sure he was doing the right thing.

FOUR

Doctor Maxim Rachman was a professor of psychology at Taras Shevchenko National University in Kyiv.

He looked out his office window and thought about his life and all that had gone wrong.

It was rainy, and the clouds were a light grey, almost white. He wished he was somewhere else. It always seemed to be raining in Kyiv. The locals often joked that it was due to the fallout from Chernobyl, which was only one hundred miles away.

Maxim sighed.

His day job at the university was just a cover. A ruse.

It'd been that way for years.

He was a phony, and he was abusing his knowledge.

When he first became a doctor, his primary area of study focused on soldiers who had acute PTSD, men and women who'd experienced immense trauma and had been mentally shutdown. For years, he was known as one of the leading figures in the subject. He lectured about it worldwide. His papers were cited regularly.

His most famous paper was entitled, 'Deciphering the inner psyche of the soldier: *Breaking them down using therapeutic hallucinogenics.*' His research was comprised of endless interviews with current and ex-soldiers. With some government moderation, he administered a cocktail of drugs into the interviewees' veins. In their heightened states, he'd ask them questions. He'd get them to open up in ways that, if they were lucid, they never would. In short, he'd get them to talk by placing them in a subconscious state. He'd heal their minds.

The study was mostly financed by the Ukrainian government and military through a variety of grants. At first, he didn't think much of the money he was given. He simply thought those in positions of power wanted to understand why some of the soldiers who fought for the country suffered from mental illness and how they could better treat them—it seemed altruistic. His work was about helping those in need, nothing more.

However, shortly after the paper was published, he was brought to the Temny Facility. It was there that he realized the military's funding was for reasons other than altruistic purposes.

They didn't care about their soldiers' well-being.

In Temny, he met with Commander Oksi, who told Maxim that he'd called the meeting because he wanted to know if Maxim wanted to *help*. He was a fan of Maxim's work, apparently.

"I don't know what *help* means?" Maxim said. "Can you elaborate?"

Oksi told the two armed guards who'd escorted Maxim from the parking garage to leave the room. Once they were gone, Oksi elaborated. "I want you to work for the military," he said. "I've read your papers—all of them. I'm the reason your work has been funded. You've been studying soldiers and their minds your whole academic life. You know how to break them down. You know what it takes to get them to talk."

"I'm still not following," Maxim said. "Do you want me to provide therapy for the soldiers stationed at this facility?"

"What I am about to tell you must stay between us," Oksi said. "I want you to work as an interrogator. I want you to break the minds of the men and women we bring in. I want you to get them to talk. We hold high-profile military prisoners here."

"I'm not a trained interrogator. I wouldn't know where to begin. My whole area of study has been focused on helping soldiers—

helping them navigate the difficult transition back to civilian life after their service has ended. They want to talk to me. That's how I help them."

"You drug them."

"With their consent."

"Consent won't matter with the people you interrogate here," Oksi said. "Your knowledge in this area of study is unmatched. You could really help us. Tensions with Russia are high, and there are various rebel groups in Crimea and other parts of our country that are making life difficult. I worry about war every day. You could help prevent one."

"I'm not interested."

Oksi smiled. "Perhaps I am not making myself clear ..." He cracked his knuckles and leaned back in his chair. "You are going to help us. You will interview the men I tell you to interview. You will drug them and try to get them to answer a series of specific questions."

"We can't administer drugs to prisoners without their consent."

"We can, and we will. We will do what we must do."

"You've read my papers. Why don't you administer the drugs yourself? I'll tell you everything—"

"You know the mind," Oksi said. "You are a psychologist. You know the questions to ask—you have mastered the approach. I could read a million books about flying an aircraft, but I wouldn't really know how to fly one. There's a physical feeling one gets when doing a job. You could read a book about firing a gun, yet I know the actual act of pulling down on a physical trigger would scare you. You'd forget what you read. Listen, I can see that you're scared, but you need to understand that I'm giving you the opportunity of a lifetime. All you have to do is administer your drugs, talk to the men we bring into this facility, and get them to talk. It'll be no different than the study I made sure the government funded."

"I can't," Maxim said. "It's too far out of my space. I am an academic. I am not a soldier. I do not belong in the military. You would—"

"You would still be an academic," Oksi said. "Your day job would remain the same. I would only need you when we have someone who won't talk. You'd be a last resort of sorts. I would only call on you after we've exhausted more traditional avenues of interrogation. When all else fails, if we can't get them to talk by breaking down their bodies, then we will break down their minds."

"I am not comfortable with this."

"You don't have to be."

"I'm sorry, I have to decline."

"You don't have a choice."

"This is absurd."

"Need I repeat that the military funded your papers? We provided you with access to our men. Did you think that didn't come with a cost? Your career would not exist without the Ukrainian Government's investment. If you decline this invitation, I assure you that you will not like what happens next. I could make your life miserable. You have a family, no?"

Maxim understood the threat. It wasn't just his career that would be destroyed.

He had no choice. He nodded and left the facility.

His knowledge was being used against him.

After leaving Temny that first day, he walked through the streets of Kyiv for hours. He'd be lying if he denied that a part of him wasn't intrigued by the idea of helping the military—the thought of all that access to all that information—but when he considered the cost, it seemed like too much. He'd become a psychologist to help people, not to break them down.

As he ate dinner that night, his wife looked anxiously at him. His two-year-old daughter, wonderfully ignorant to all his inner turmoil, smiled. Maxim wanted to cry.

"What's wrong?" Josephina asked.

"Nothing," he said.

"Is this about your brother? What did Roman do now?"

"No, it's not about him."

"I haven't seen you this upset since Roman took all that money from you."

"It's not about Roman."

Maxim went to bed that night and wondered when he'd get the first call from Commander Oksi.

It took three days.

It was just like Oksi had said it would be. When the military couldn't get a subject to talk, Maxim would be called in. He would meet with the subject, analyze them, and administer them hallucinogenic drugs as they were strapped to a table. Thirty minutes later, when the effects of the drug took effect, he'd begin his questioning.

He'd pull what he could from them.

Sometimes it worked, sometimes it didn't.

His approach usually centered around talking about their families, their failures, their successes. He'd build up a profile and, when he had enough information, he'd turn on them—he'd unleash on them a nightmare of their subconscious.

By the time he was done interrogating, they'd be in tears.

He hated that.

He'd lecture at the university in the day, and when Commander Oksi called, he'd tell his wife that he'd be coming home late. She never asked him what he was doing—the money was good, and Maxim, though sometimes sad, seemed satisfied.

Maxim didn't know what happened to the men after the *interrogation*. All he knew about his subjects were the basics.

"This man knows the leader of a terrorist cell," Oksi would say. "We've tortured him, but he won't talk. Do what you do best!"

Maxim would enter the holding cell, administer the drugs, and do his job.

For three years, that was what he did.

Looking out the window of his university office, Maxim thought about his options. On his computer screen was an unopened email from Oksi. It'd been six months since the last time they'd communicated. He knew what he'd discover if he opened the email.

He'd be brought to Temny.

He looked back at his computer and felt hopeless.

He opened the email. Oski wanted to chat.

Maxim replied to the email and hit send.

Five minutes later, his phone rang.

"I need you to come to Temny tomorrow morning. There is a job for you," Oksi said. "This guy won't break."

"I'll be there."

"Good."

Maxim closed his briefcase and left his office. He got inside his BMW 3 Series Sedan and left the campus. On his way home, he called his wife.

"Did you know your brother was stopping by?" she said as she answered.

"What? Roman? No. Is he there?"

"You need to come home," she said. "You need to tell him to leave."

"I told him to stay away from the house. Did he say why he came?"

"He wanted to personally thank you for getting him the job."

Maxim rubbed his brow—one problem on top of another. His younger brother was a nuisance in almost every way. "Tell him to meet me at The Old Communist bar. Tell him I'll pay for his tab. He can thank me there. Just get him out of the house."

"Ok, my love," Josephina said.

Maxim hung up and grunted in frustration. He had been looking forward to a relaxing night with his wife and child. Instead, he'd be dealing with the man-child that was his brother.

And under the surface of it all was the reminder that tomorrow he'd be betraying his knowledge. He'd interrogate a vulnerable subject. Instead of helping those in need, he'd take advantage of them.

FIVE

Drake wiped his brow. It was more than hot. He'd grown up in southern Texas but had never experienced anything like the humid heat of a Thailand summer. It weighed on you, held you down, and compressed your lungs. It sometimes hurt to breathe.

He and Pok had been following the tourist for more than an hour.

The tourist finally came to a stop outside of a hotel named The Golden Flower. It was a popular spot in Sansor for those who had illicit interests. Its halls and rooms were full of vermin, mostly of the human kind. If there was trouble in the village, it was guaranteed to start or end at The Golden Flower.

"What now?" Pok said. "What are we even doing? Once he's in that hotel, he'll be able to do whatever he wants to the girl. We should have stopped him."

"Shhh!" Drake said, not looking down at Pok. He kept his gaze on the tourist.

The two of them were standing beside a flower shop across the street from the hotel. A cluster of about thirty motorized rickshaws and taxicabs were between them and their target. It was noisy, and the smell of exhaust filled the air.

"I'm going to return the wallet," Drake said.

Pok looked confused. "Wait, what? We traveled all this way just to return his wallet? I thought you said you wanted to teach this guy a lesson!"

"Hold on to this," Drake said. He handed Pok the small package he'd picked up from the post office. "Watch what I do. Learn from it. If you want to stop guys like this from coming to Sansor, this is how you'll keep them out."

Pok took the package.

Drake crossed the street. He pushed through the cluster of rickshaws and cabs. A haze of smoke surrounded The Golden Flower, on account of the dozens or so unsavory people outside smoking weed, cigarettes, or cigars.

The tourist they'd been tracking was whispering into the ear of one of the unsavory figures. The young girl at his side could barely stand. Her legs wobbled.

The tourist was paying for his room. He let go of his grip on the girl's wrist and reached for his wallet. His sausage-like fingers struggled to dig deep into his tight shorts. He fumbled nervously inside his pants—where was it? A panicked look struck his face. It wasn't one of mortal danger, though. He'd be fine without his cards. All he'd have to do was call his bank, and they'd send new ones over. What panicked him was the fact that he wanted her. He'd just popped a few pills. He needed her soon. He could feel the bulge in his shorts.

Drake approached the tourist and pulled out his wallet.

"Are you looking for this?" he said.

The tourist immediately recognized the American accent and turned around. When he saw Drake, his eyes widened. Drake towered over him.

"Why, yes," the tourist said, noticing the wallet in Drake's hand. "Thank you." He reached for his wallet.

Drake didn't hand it over. He looked at the girl, then back at the tourist. "She looks young?"

The tourist fixed his glasses. His skin perspired to the point that the glasses wouldn't stay on his face. His hands shook as he pushed his glasses back up. "Can I have my wallet, please!" He tried to sound authoritative.

Drake handed him the wallet.

The tourist took it and looked inside. He looked up at Drake. "Hey, where's the money?"

"Finder's fee," Drake said. "I gave it to the kid who picked it from your back pocket."

"What?" The tourist was confused.

"Hey," the unsavory figure said, interrupting Drake and the tourist's conversation. He grabbed the tourist by the arm. "You want a room? I need money. Pay now!"

The tourist turned from Drake back to the man he had been speaking to earlier. He was beginning to sweat badly. Thick droplets fell from his forehead and splashed against the concrete. "I don't have any cash."

"You don't need cash," the man said. "I accept all major credit cards. This is the twenty-first-century." He smiled, revealing a mouth of gold-plated teeth.

"Excellent!" the tourist said. He grabbed one of his credit cards— the gold one. The one that gave him free travel insurance and cash-back points.

"Thank you. I'll charge the card and get you the key to the room." The unsavory man walked into the hotel to charge the card.

THE TOURIST LOOKED at the young girl he'd picked up from Phuket. She looked ripe. She was ready. He turned back to confront Drake. He wanted to give the tall American a piece of his mind before he had his fun.

"Now, listen—" He froze.

The tall American was gone.

The tourist felt his heart pound in his chest. He could feel his fingers tingle. Did his heart skip a beat? Was he losing feeling? He looked left and right down the busy street. Had it all just been a dream? Was he letting his paranoia get to him? Was the man even real? Did he lose his wallet?

He looked down at the child he'd bought. "Did you see him?" he asked her.

She was too drugged to recognize the question. And even if she wasn't drugged, she only understood a few simple sentences in English.

The unsavory man walked out of the hotel. "I've got the room. Here is your receipt."

The tourist snatched the receipt out of the man's hand, stuffed it in his pocket, grabbed hold of the child's wrist, and walked up to the hotel's entrance. He stopped.

Something was wrong.

The street outside the hotel seemed to wake up in a flurry of noise. Cars honked, the rickshaw drivers yelled and hollered at each other. The thick and reverberating sounds of engines and screams ricocheted off the tall buildings that swallowed the street.

Was that a police siren?

The tourist wanted to escape. He just wanted to take advantage of the girl. He wanted what he'd come to Thailand to do. He pulled her violently to the entrance, yanking her wrist so hard that she fell over.

"You stupid bitch!" he snapped.

He turned around to pick her up. She was out cold. The drugs had finally taken over. He dropped the bag of trinkets he'd bought for his kids back in Seattle. He tried to pull her up. She was like a dead weight.

Suddenly, thick, muscular hands grabbed him. He felt six hands at least. They pulled him down, tackling him to the concrete. His glasses fell off. Everything was a blur. He looked up into the blue sky. He wanted to yell, but the wind had been knocked out of his lungs. He could hardly speak. The police snatched the receipt out of the tourist's pocket.

DRAKE APPEARED BESIDE POK AGAIN. He grabbed the package from Pok's hands.

"You wanted him to pay for the room?" Pok asked.

"I wanted him to use one of his cards."

"He'll be in trouble."

"He'll be in a lot of trouble."

"I see."

"It'll send a message," Drake grunted. "But no matter how many weeds you prune, there'll always be more."

"I think I get it," Pok said.

Drake turned and walked back to the market and his cabin by the beach.

"Where are you going?" Pok asked.

"Home," Drake said. "I need to rest. I need to clear my head."

"You're a good man, Mr. Drake. You remind me of my brother."

Drake stopped. "You had a brother?"

"He died. He was ten years older than me. He wanted to be a police officer. He got sick, though. He died. You are like him. That's why I help you."

"I had a brother, too," Drake said. "Stay safe, kid."

"Will do," Pok said.

He watched Drake disappear down an alley and then turned back to the action outside the hotel. The Thai police had the tourist in handcuffs. The young girl he was with was being put into the front seat of a police car. There were about twenty officers on the scene. The whole street seemed chaotic.

"I didn't know her age," the tourist screamed. "She said she was eighteen! I swear! I swear!"

The plump American was jammed in the back of a police car. His screams stopped when the cops shut the door.

Pok smiled.

He couldn't wait to try that technique on the next child predator that came through the streets of Sansor.

SIX

"Where to, Madam Director?" the driver of the limo asked.

"Home," Price said. She was in the backseat of the limo. "I need a drink. I've just been fired."

"Of course, ma'am."

It'd been minutes since her intelligence brief with the President. Minutes since he'd privately let her know he was firing her.

Her world was about to change.

The driver pulled out of the oval driveway in front of the White House and turned onto Pennsylvania Avenue. He drove Price toward her townhouse in Kalorama—the expensive and exclusive neighborhood in Northwest DC.

The neighborhood had been home to some of the highest-profile members of the US government. Woodrow Wilson had lived there until three years before his death—soon after which, his house had been designated a National Historic Landmark.

As the ornate and illustrious buildings of Kalorama passed, Price began to feel a sense of dread.

What was she going to do now? Since the late eighties, all she had known was the CIA. It had been her whole adult life. Would she get a consulting job for some private security firm? Or a job at a think tank?

The limo came to a stop outside her house. Kate thanked the driver and stepped out.

She went inside and tossed her overcoat on the long table that hugged the wall of her front hallway. She made her way to the wine rack in her kitchen and grabbed a bottle of red. It was a 2012 Cabernet Sauvignon. She'd been saving it for a special day.

Before opening the bottle, she checked the clock. It was 16:15 PM.

"It's five o'clock somewhere," she muttered. She uncorked the bottle and poured herself a glass.

"You're home early," Clyde Colt said.

He'd just stepped out of the shower wearing a white shower robe. He'd just shaved, but he'd left his signature mustache in place. It glistened with tiny droplets of water. Colt had been growing his hair long, and he had it slicked back. He smelled of aftershave.

Colt was a fifty-eight-year-old Scottish former-SAS officer and Kate's ex-husband. They'd split up after their ten-year-old died of cancer, but life's many strange journeys had brought them back together. The two had been living with each other on and off for the last three years. Colt would fly back to London every now and then—training assignments with the SAS, he said. Price didn't mind his coming and going. She just liked that he was around.

Price took a sip of her wine and wiped her mouth. "I've been fired," she said.

"You serious?" Colt asked. He wasn't surprised. The smile on his face made that evident.

She took another gulp of wine and nodded.

He burst out laughing.

"What's funny?" she asked.

"I'm surprised you lasted this long," he said. "You weren't ever fit for that job."

"You're a dick."

"And you're too much of a pain in the ass."

She angrily punched his arm and put her empty glass down. "Is that supposed to make me feel better?"

Colt embraced her. He held her tight, kissed her forehead, and said, "It will be okay, love."

"I really hate you sometimes."

"Why's that?"

"Because you're the only one in this whole damn world who seems to understand me."

"Aye, I am. And I'm tellin' you the truth. You were better in the field, out where it mattered. Seeing you cooped up all day in an office, surrounded by sycophants, depressed me. You can't make a difference from inside those walls."

"President Clarkson is a fool. He's afraid to get messy. He's changed."

"He's a politician," Colt said. "All that matters to him is his image. Nothing more. He might have started out as a business man, but he's been in Washington a long time. He had to change. Maybe just to keep his sanity about him. He's scared, Kate. He's just trying to stick to the safest path."

"That safe path could give Russia a good chunk of Europe. It'll be like the Cold War all over again. If Ukraine falls, then it's only a matter of time before Slovakia, the Czech Republic. Russian hegemony over the region will be vast and swift. It just takes one domino to fall, you know that. And President Clarkson is going to let them do it by not sending our troops to Ukraine, by not forcing them to back down. It's going to be a mess, and we're going to come out weaker on the other end."

"NATO won't let them do that," Colt said. "You could be overreacting."

"You know as well as I do that the combined militaries of Germany, France, and the United Kingdom wouldn't even come close to Russia's. We need to stop this fire before it spreads. Europe still needs us."

"Well, it won't be your problem soon."

"I have one week."

"He gave you a week?"

"He wants me to find my replacement."

"And is that what you're going to do?"

"I have direct orders from the President not to get involved in Ukraine. I'll find the replacement."

"You should listen to him," Colt said. "Don't be foolish. Not many of us are given an easy way out, love."

"I'll do what I have to do," she said.

The two of them looked at each other and tried not to think about anything outside the kitchen, though both their minds wavered from that simple task.

Colt grabbed the bottle of wine from the counter and a glass from the cupboard. He poured himself a healthy glass. He drank it back. "I leave for London tomorrow. Graham Howe—the pecker—he's opened a new training facility close to Manchester. He wants me to look it over. You could come with me?"

"I need to do what the President asked," she said, snuggling her head into his shoulder. "Maybe in a week. I need to find my replacement."

He kissed her. She turned around and kissed him back. The two of them closed their eyes and embraced each other's warmth.

They walked slowly up the stairs to her bedroom, where they made love like they used to. They'd been through so much together that they knew they could take on anything. Even this.

SEVEN

The street lights flickered on as Maxim stepped out of his car. Outside it was raining. He stuck two coins into the meter beside the curb and walked to the Old Communist to meet his brother.

The bar was three miles from his house and was one of the newer bars in the city. It was located between a barbershop and an art store and had an excellent Pilsner selection. Maxim liked it because it wasn't inhabited by locals. Most of the people who drank there were ex-pats: American, British, or Canadian.

When he drank there, they left him alone.

He stepped inside the bar and looked for Roman, his asshole brother.

"Over here!"

Maxim turned in the direction of the voice.

There he was. Roman. He nodded to his brother and pushed through the bar's patrons. He sat down at the booth his brother had chosen.

"I told you never to go to my house."

"I am just thankful, brother," Roman said. "You helped me when I was at my lowest. I wanted to thank you in person."

"You are my blood. That is why I helped you," Maxim said. "That is the only reason. I don't need your thanks."

"Let me buy you a drink," Roman said. "It's the least I can do."

"I know very well you don't have the money," Maxim said. He looked at the empty glasses on the table. "Josephina told you I would take care of the tab, didn't she? How much have you drunk?"

"Just one."

"The three empty glasses suggest otherwise."

"They were here before I sat down." Roman burped.

Maxim rolled his eyes. "Blyat," he said under his breath.

Both Maxim and Roman grew up in Kyiv during the dawn of democracy in Ukraine. They were teenagers in the mid-eighties when all the big changes were going down. Their father had been a general in the Russian army and had died when they were young, leaving only their mother to care for the two boys through a tumultuous period of Eastern European history. Thankfully, due to Ukraine's close ties with the West, the country's transition from Soviet satellite state to a democratic country was one of relative calm —calm only relative to other Eastern Bloc countries.

Things in the Rachman household were never as calm as the country's transition between two types of political control. The two brothers were different. So different, they often butted heads.

Maxim did well in school. Roman did not. Roman made friends with everyone, even the most undesirable kinds. Maxim didn't have any friends. This dichotomy came to a head after the death of their mother.

It was just before Maxim went off to study at Cambridge University—three years after the fall of the Berlin Wall. The two of them had just left the funeral.

"I need some money," Roman said to his brother.

They walked outside the old church. It was a sunny day. Maxim hated that.

"I don't have any money."

Roman looked at his brother and shook his head. "Don't lie, brother. I know you have money. How else would you be paying for the tuition in that expensive university in England?"

"With hard work and a scholarship."

"I need some of that scholarship money. I'll pay you back."

"I won't—"

Roman sucker-punched his brother in the temple and grabbed some money Maxim had in his wallet.

Days later, Roman showed up at Maxim's apartment and handed his brother a five hundred-euro note.

"I'm sorry," he said. "I was desperate. How's your head?"

Maxim took the money and slammed the door. He didn't speak to his brother for a decade. He went off to England and became a psychologist.

After securing tenure at the university, Roman reappeared.

"I need help," he said, standing in Maxim's doorway.

"How did you find me?"

"You always wanted to live in Perchesk—the most expensive and richest area in town. I knew you'd do well in school. And I knew you'd look for a home around here. You like the attention."

"Screw you, brother. You robbed me the last time we spoke."

"I won't ever rob you again."

"How can I believe you?"

"I, too, have become rich."

"Yet you need my help?"

"I'll pay you good money. I just need a place to hide out."

"If I refuse?" Maxim asked.

"Then I will die."

Maxim let Roman in—after dinner, when Jospehina had gone to bed. Roman told Maxim what he'd been up to. The trouble he was in.

"A deal went wrong," he said. "I never wanted any part of it. Russian gangsters were involved. They backstabbed my partner. They killed him."

"You idiot," Maxim said.

"You know I wouldn't have come back here if it wasn't serious. I know you hate my guts. You have every reason to. I'm sorry."

"Leave."

Roman went to leave the house but stopped at the door. A black SUV was parked across the street. One of the windows was rolled down. Tiny barrels were stuck out of the dark window.

"Get down!" Roman yelled, tackling his brother, who was standing beside him at the door.

Thunderous explosions roared from the open windows. Bullets chewed up the front facade of Maxim's house.

The car drove off.

"They were following you!" Maxim yelled. "You moron!"

"I told you I need help."

"You're lying!" Maxim said.

"Okay, okay," Roman said. "Maybe the Russian gangsters didn't betray me. Maybe I betrayed them. Look—I need money. I owe them thirty thousand euros."

"What?"

"And now that they know where you live ... well, I'm sorry, brother. But you're in this as much as I am."

"You asshole."

Maxim had no choice. He gave his brother the money and told him that he never wanted to see him again. Roman took the money, paid off the gangsters and disappeared.

And for fifteen years, Roman stayed out of Maxim's life.

It'd been such a long time that Maxim thought maybe his brother had died. When Roman finally showed up again, looking older, he gave his brother a hug. Time had healed some of the pain, neutered some of the memory. Maxim knew it wasn't just that, though. He felt guilty. How could he hate his brother when, in his mind, he was no different? He'd taken the money from the government. He injected drugs into men and women without their consent and asked them questions to break them down. He was a bad man.

So when his brother showed up again asking for help, Maxim helped him. This time without question. He got his brother a job at Temny. He told Commander Oksi that it was non-negotiable. Oksi didn't mind. The facility needed a new janitor.

Maxim stared at his brother. The dim lights of the bar made Roman look weak and frail. "You need to stay away from my house."

"I'm sorry," Roman said. "I am just very thankful. When I showed up at your door three weeks ago, you had no reason to help me. I just wanted to thank you for the job."

"And how does it feel to earn your money honestly?"

"I love it. Brother, I love you. I... I am forever in your debt."

The waitress appeared and asked Maxim if he wanted a drink. He declined. "Just get me the bill."

"You won't have one drink with me?" Roman asked.

"No," Maxim said. "I have an early morning. I'll be visiting Temny."

"I'll see you tomorrow, then," Roman said, a wide smile on his face—almost to the point of desperation.

"Just sober yourself up," Maxim said. "Drink lots of water when you go home. If you lose that job, I won't be able to help you."

"Of course."

"And if you ever show up at my house again, I'll ..." Maxim shook his head in anger. "Just don't show up at my house."

"Of course."

Maxim paid the bill and went home.

He slowly walked into his house.

One of the things he'd learned in school was never to psychoanalyze yourself. It's an impossible task, yet he couldn't help himself.

Did he help his brother simply because of the guilt? Was he trying to be a good person?

He kissed his daughter goodnight and crawled into bed next to Josephina.

He'd wake up in the morning and betray his oath to help those in need. He'd administer drugs to a prisoner and torture their mind.

EIGHT

Drake went back to his beach cabin and opened up the package. Inside was a passport and ten thousand American dollars.

She'd come through.

He now had what he needed to go home. Dallas? Austin? Which city would he hit first? Both he knew well.

She'd also left him a note.

> J.,
>
> Here's the passport. It wasn't easy to get.
> I hope you're okay.
> Your friend misses you.
> You know who.

He smiled, put the letter on his table, and grabbed a beer from the fridge. He walked outside onto the porch and sat on a wicker chair. He sipped the beer slowly and listened to the sounds of the ocean waves crashing against the shore. His eyes felt heavy.

What Pok had told him had stuck with him. He didn't know he and the kid had so much in common.

Dead brothers. Lost. Gone.

He closed his eyes. He needed rest. The beer fell out of his hand and spilled onto the wooden floorboards. He didn't notice.

He then heard a loud explosion. It sounded like a gunshot.

He shot up from his chair. His eyes widened; he stood ready. His heart pounding, he quickly found the source of the sound.

Drunk teenagers down by the beach were setting off fireworks. The sparkling, colorful remnants of the explosion fell toward the black of the water.

Drake shook his head and rubbed his eyes. "Shit," he said, noticing his spilled beer.

He picked up the bottle and went back into his cabin. He drank a glass of water and then laid down on his bed.

He tried not to think about his past or his future. He just wanted to focus on the sound of the the waves.

But Drake knew his past was gaining on him. He'd been running for too long. It was chasing him down. He was being hunted, cornered, trapped.

He couldn't keep hiding.

As he drifted off to sleep, thoughts of his past turned into a nightmare.

He dreamed of the night his brother left.

"I'm leaving town," Colin Drake said. The nineteen-year-old stuffed a pile of wrinkled white t-shirts into a duffel bag and then looked at his twelve-year-old brother—Drake—who was standing at the doorway to his room. "I'm done with this place."

"Leaving?"

"Yes," Colin said. "I hate it here." He paused and corrected himself. "I'm just leaving, alright." He looked out of his bedroom window. "I'll stay in contact, little bro. Don't you worry. This will be good for you."

Drake looked up at his brother with a dismayed expression. "When Mom finds out, you'll be dead—you won't be able to come back."

Colin looked at his little brother and smiled. "Mom doesn't give a shit about me."

"She does!"

"She doesn't." Colin's face was lit up in the glow of the moon that shone through his bedroom window. "She doesn't care about you either, but you'll learn that, too, one day. She's a damn monster."

"So, you're just going to leave me, then," Drake said. "You're going to leave me with a monster?"

"You'll be fine with Mom for the time being. It'll toughen you up. Thicken your skin. But when the time comes, don't be afraid to do what you have to do. Understand?"

Drake looked at Colin and shook his head. "What are you even talking about?"

"Mom's been a drunk since Dad died. If I could deal with it for a couple of years, so can you—but you need to keep your wits about you. She's a relentless bitch."

Drake grabbed his brother's arm. "Dave is an asshole. Is that why you're leaving? Are you afraid of him?"

Dave was their mom's new boyfriend—a car salesman from Dallas.

"He's part of the reason why I need to go," Colin said with a shrug. "I don't want to hurt him. If I stay here long enough, I'll end up in juvie."

"You're an asshole," Drake said.

"Ah, shut up, bro. Before I leave, do you want to help me leave Dave a message?"

"What message?"

"Let's scratch his Mercedes."

"Is this a smart thing to do?"

"Smart thing? We're two kids who grew up in a messed-up home. I failed every test a teacher ever gave me—I have nothing. I have no future. One day, you'll learn what that means. You'll know what I'm talking about. You'll understand why I'm leaving. I don't care about doing the smart thing. You get it?"

"So, we're just going to key his car?"

"Yes."

"And then what?"

"I don't know."

Drake shook his head. "Will you write? Will you keep me posted?"

"Of course. Trust me." Colin winked at his little brother.

Drake looked out the window. Stars dotted Austin's skyline. The branches of nearby trees didn't shake. The world felt still.

"You gonna help?" Colin said.

Drake looked up at his brother and nodded. He just wanted to spend more time with Colin. That was his justification.

The two brothers made their way out of the room quietly. They tiptoed down the hallway, the stairs, and through the living room. They both froze when they saw the silhouette of Dave's head above the top of the couch. Drake crouched low and made his way closer to the large man their mother had been dating for over six months.

He looked over Dave's shoulder. The bastard was sleeping. A thick glob of drool dripped from his mouth and was pooling on his shirt. There were six empty bottles of beer on the coffee table and a burned-out cigarette in his hand. The television was repeating infomercials about some new type of can opener.

He made his way back to his brother. "He's passed out," he said. "But we have to be careful."

"You need to relax."

"Why do you want to do this?" Drake asked.

"Because this is the fucker who's been sleeping with our Mom. He's pushing her into madness."

"We ..." Drake tried to think of something to say to his brother to get him to change his mind, but his brother was telling him the truth.

The two brothers made their way outside. Crickets chirped, and the trees seemed motionless.

Drake was still in his socks.

The Mercedes was in the driveway—it glistened from the light of a streetlamp. It was a beautiful vehicle. It was meant to attract attention.

Colin picked up two stones from the garden. He handed one to Drake. "Make sure you blame me," he said. "I don't want you taking any of the blame for this."

"I'll do what I have to do," Drake said. He was feeling more adventurous now. If there was one thing Colin knew how to do, it was make him feel alive, make him push his boundaries, even if it felt stupid to do so.

Colin smiled. "I'm going to miss you, Jason," he said. "It's a damn shame Dad died when he did. You would have really liked him."

Their father died before Drake's third birthday. He grew up never really knowing his father.

"You just promise me that you'll keep in touch."

"I already told you that I would."

"Then what are we waiting for?" Drake said. He jammed the stone Colin had handed him against the chassis of the car and slid it across its body. It etched a thick, deep groove in the paintwork, one that would be very expensive to repair. Colin laughed and did the same.

The two brothers marked up the car in their juvenile act of rebellion.

"I'm going to make sure this asshole knows it was me," Colin said. He began to carve his name into the bonnet. "I want this asshole to regret ever meeting our mom."

Drake laughed and then noticed something at the window. From the corner of his eye, he saw the light of the television turn off. Inside the house, he saw the dark shape of Dave stumble.

"Shhh!" he said to Colin, who hadn't yet noticed. "He's up!"

Colin didn't hear Drake's hushed voice. He just kept giggling and scratching up the expensive vehicle.

Drake crouched and made his way to his brother. He grabbed Colin's hand. "You need to stop," he said.

"What is it?"

"He's up!"

Colin leered around the vehicle and looked through the front window of the house. The living room television set had been turned off.

"He's probably grabbing another beer."

"You need to go," Drake said. "We've done enough damage. He'll get the point."

"No!" Colin said. "This asshole took our mother from us. He

brainwashed her. Broke her. Did you see those bruises on her arm? He hurts her."

Drake closed his eyes. He didn't want to think about the pain his mother had endured simply so that she could have a man who could provide for her family.

"I want this asshole to know I hate him!" Colin said.

"And what about Mom? She's going to be the one Dave blames for this."

"Is that such a bad thing?"

"Our mother is sad," Drake said. "We can't—"

Colin cut him off. "You need to stop feeling sorry for her. She did this to herself. I thought you were stronger than this. I thought you were cooler. Don't be a damn coward. If you want to run back inside, then go run back inside. Just know that if you do, I won't stay in touch."

Drake looked into his brother's eyes. "Okay," he said. "I'm sorry."

"Good," Colin said.

After five more minutes of vandalization, Colin whistled. Drake stopped what he was doing and made his way to his brother.

"I think we're done."

"What now?" Drake asked.

"Now—well, now you go back inside, and I finish what I started."

"What are you going to do?"

"I'm going to set this thing on fire."

"Don't be stupid," Drake said. "You could hurt yourself! You could—"

"Shut up!" Colin said. "I'm lying. I'm just going to smash the windshield. You're so easy to fool."

"How will you get away?" Drake said. "He's up. If he hears a thing, he'll run after you."

"I stole a motorbike," Colin said.

"What?"

"Look."

Drake turned toward the street and saw a small Kawasaki motorcycle. "Where'd you get that thing?"

"I stole it. I'm going to miss you, buddy. Just go inside, and when you hear the window smash and the engine fire up, don't come looking for me."

The two brothers embraced in the shadow of the expensive car.

"Stay safe," Drake said.

"I'll be fine," Colin said.

Drake made his way back into the house. His eyes were damp, his heart pounded. He was too young to fully understand the complex emotions he was feeling. He was angry at himself, his brother, Dave, his mother, and his father all at once. The whole world seemed against him, and he didn't truly know how to grasp it.

He was so lost in emotion that he didn't notice the two thick legs in front of the entrance of the house. He froze, looked up, and saw Dave smiling. The large man was holding a beer and shaking his head.

"I knew you boys had it in for me," he growled. "I'm going to make sure that you both end up in juvie for this!"

Drake turned back to his brother and yelled, "Colin! Run!"

Colin looked up from behind the Mercedes and saw his brother's warning.

Somehow, despite his drunken buffoonery, Dave tackled Drake and held him down. The two of them rolled onto a flowerbed.

"Stop!" Colin shouted.

Drake's face was jammed against the soil. He could hardly hear his brother, let alone breathe.

Dave looked up. "You little shits are going to pay! I should just kill you!"

Colin smashed the front window of the vehicle.

"You little shit!" Dave's voice was so guttural, the words were hardly intelligible. He pushed himself upright. Drake seized the opportunity to roll to cover. He gasped for air.

"Come back here!" Dave howled, running after Colin.

"Screw you!" Colin shouted, hopping atop his motorcycle.

Dave's words slurred. "You little shits don't understand a damn thing! The only reason I'm fucking your mother is your father's pension! A dead cop gets paid a pretty penny in this state. You little assholes are trying to screw me out of money, and I won't have that. I'll make sure you both regret this!"

Colin's eyes widened to the point that he seemed completely out of control. He started up the motorcycle and drove off. The bike's tires screeched along the blacktop.

There were half a dozen people standing on their lawns watching the conflict. It was just another night in suburbia.

Dave turned back to Drake.

His steps were long. The ground seemed to shake when he moved.

Drake woke up from his nightmare. He was covered in sweat.

It was four a.m. He pushed himself up and stretched. He did twenty push-ups and left his cabin. The stars outside shone brightly and lit up the waves that stretched to the horizon.

He needed to go for a run.

He took off his shoes and walked down the steps of the cabin's porch to the beach. His toes dug into the sand. He ran towards the water. He knew it was the only way he'd be able to clear his head.

He did everything he could to not think of his past.

NINE

The Temny Facility was a four-story tall fortress located in the Pechers'kyi district of Kyiv. The district is home to the Kyiv Pechersk Lavra monastery complex, which was comprised of an intricate and lavish group of buildings and catacombs. It was one of the more populated areas of the city, full of fancy clubs, bars, and restaurants that served borscht soup and dumplings.

It was close to Maxim's house—a ten-minute drive at most.

He drove down the streets of Kyiv toward the bland, Soviet-era-style building. From the outside, it looked like a slab of concrete. A tall fence, with barbed wire at the top, surrounded the building. The entrance was guarded by four men in long coats.

Most people in Kyiv didn't know what happened within the walls of the complex. Anyone who noticed the unusual building assumed that it was just another government office.

Maxim rolled down his window as he approached the gate and sighed when he saw a young military officer approach his car. It was early morning and still dark out. The sky was clear and slowly turning orange. The officer manning the gate was young and looked fresh out of boot camp.

"Would it hurt for any of you guys to hold this job for more than a couple of months?" Maxim said as he flashed his security card. "If one of you actually stuck around for some time, I wouldn't have to go through this whole song and dance."

The officer snapped the card out of Maxim's hands and scanned it with his reader. He walked back to his stall, made some calls, and, after confirming everything was okay, walked back to Maxim.

"You're good to go," the guard said as he handed Maxim back his card. "I'll open the door for you." He walked back to his booth and hit the switch to open the gate.

Only one guard stood at the gate, and he was unarmed. This was to avoid attracting unnecessary attention from those on the street. Plus, if anyone broke in, there were enough armed guards within to take care of any hostile intruder quickly.

Irritated, Maxim waited for the metal gates to open. He drove inside. He shook his head and cursed under his breath as he steered his way through the complex.

He drove into the underground parking garage and parked in the spot designated for him.

He got out of his car, made his way to the elevator, and scanned his security card through the reader. He waited for the elevator door to open, got inside, and, beholden to the overly secure nature of the facility, scanned his card again. Once the small light turned green above the floor buttons, he hit the floor for Commander Oksi's office and waited for the door to close.

So much of the facility was operated by technology. This was on account of Oksi. He was paranoid.

Since the facility housed some of the most wanted men in Ukraine, he wanted to be able to lock down the facility at a moment's notice. It was one of the reasons why security cameras and biometric scanners were placed everywhere in the building.

Because of this, the facility was referred to as the most secure place in all of Ukraine. Adding to its secured nature, it operated on its own electrical grid. Oksi had told Maxim that fact during one of their first meetings. He was bragging about it more than informing Maxim of anything meaningful. The commander was proud that the Ukrainian military had entrusted him with the stewardship of such a prized location.

In Maxim's eyes, it was overkill. The walls that surrounded the facility and the hundred or so personnel inside who carried fully automatic rifles were more than enough of a deterrent to keep any asshole who wanted to break in at bay. The fact that the place was located in the heart of Kyiv also made the extra security features seem pointless.

Once the elevator doors opened at the top floor, Maxim made his way to Oksi's office. He walked through the dark and narrow hallways of the facility. No one escorted him. No one needed to. At this point, if you were inside, if you had passed the numerous security checkpoints without detection, then it was believed that you were safe.

Maxim knocked on Oksi's office door.

"Come in," the commander grunted.

Maxim walked inside the small office and sat down across from Oksi.

Oksi rubbed his mustache as he looked at Maxim. "We've got a man that needs interrogating," he said.

"I figured that's why you called me here."

"He's a tough nut."

"Should I repeat myself?"

"We couldn't break him."

"Get to the point."

"You sound irritated."

"A late night."

"You should be thankful," Oksi said. "I got your brother that job, after all. You should be thankful for what I have done for you."

"What do you need me to find out? What's this interrogation about?"

Commander Oksi chuckled. "We waterboarded this guy. He was a smuggler. We tried everything. I didn't want to have to go down your route. You know I never do. But he's not typical."

"What do you want to know?"

"He works for someone. We need to find out who. We need to find out who hired him to deliver a boatload of chemical weapons to Crimean rebels. Those rebels were going to use the weapons against Russian forces. That attack could have sparked an invasion."

"Anything I should know before I start?"

"He's American."

"American?"

"Yes."

The smuggler intrigued Maxim. He'd never interrogated an American before. The assignment was unusual.

"You say you don't like this job," Oksi said. "But I can see that you do. You need to accept that you're more interested in the knowledge than you are in helping people. It's tearing you up inside. The sooner you accept things, the better."

"When can we start?"

"He's waiting for you downstairs," Oksi said. "In the holding cells. My soldiers will meet you downstairs."

"I'll get him to talk," Maxim said.

He stood up and left Oksi's office.

TEN

Maxim made his way to the holding cells. He took the elevator down from Oksi's office. As the doors opened, he saw Roman. His brother held a mop.

"Brother!" Roman yelled and waved. "How are you?"

Maxim ignored his brother and followed the two guards who met him outside the elevator toward the cell with the American smuggler.

Roman shook his head. He stopped waving and looked solemnly at his mop and bucket. He got back to work.

The pathways inside the facility were circuitous. The building was old and had undergone a variety of augmentations over the years to keep it up to date. After a short walk, one of the guards held a door open for him. Maxim walked inside the room.

The smuggler was strapped to a table. His ankles and wrists were bound with thick leather straps to the sides. A heart-rate monitor was attached to his exposed chest. He looked like he was sleeping.

"Are the drugs ready?" Maxim asked the guard at the door.

"Yes," the guard said. He lifted up a briefcase from the floor, opened it, and placed it and showed it to Maxim.

Maxim looked at the small vials inside the briefcase. He lifted one up and examined it carefully. "Thank you," he said to the guard, taking the briefcase.

The guard nodded and closed the door.

The room was lit by one small light in the center. It hung above the smuggler's body. The walls in the room were grey.

Maxim sat down on a plastic chair and looked at the smuggler. He was tall and had a wide frame. He had longish hair and a mean look on his face.

Maxim placed the briefcase with the drugs on a small table. He opened it up, and went about the work of mixing together his special cocktail of drugs; a mix of psilocybin mushrooms, zoloft, ethanol, scopolamine, sodium thiopental, and amobarbital. Mixed together, the drugs created a powerful serum. He filled a small syringe with an assortment of chemicals—mixing the drugs from each vial carefully to his specific formulation. He stuck it into the smuggler's arm.

The smuggler moaned.

Maxim sat down, started a timer on his watch and waited.

While he waited for the drug's to take effect, he pulled out a notepad from his jacket pocket.

The smuggler had been rendered unconscious by the Temny guards. The wounds on his left temple were clear enough of that. It was how the guards always delivered them. It bothered Maxim, but only slightly so. The people he'd been charged to interrogate were always intimidating. He wanted them weak and injured. To get them awake faster, necessary to answer the questions he would be asking them, required him to administer more drugs. That was it.

The large man on the table in front of him awoke from his sleep.

The drugs had begun to take effect.

Maxim wasted no time. "Who are you?" he asked in English.

"I am..." the man said slowly. His body moving left and right on the table. He had a thick accent. "I am... My name is Colin." He mumbled his words.

Maxim wrote down the name the smuggler mumbled and noted the accent. Was it Texan?

"Are you okay?" Maxim asked.

"No."

"What's wrong?"

The smuggler's eyes opened. He tried to move but couldn't. "I can't move..."

"Why are you here?"

"I don't know."

"Do you have any family?"

"I don't know."

"You don't know?" Maxim asked. His voice was soft and reassuring. He sounded like a concerned parent.

"No."

"I can help you."

The smuggler moaned. His eyes opened and closed. At times, his body violently shook. He was fighting off the drugs, or trying to. He was like a wild animal, yet to be tamed. "Did you drug me?"

"Yes."

"What's this about?"

"Tell me about your family," Maxim said.

"I don't have a family."

"We all have a family."

"Not me."

"What do you mean?" Maxim asked.

The smuggler growled. "To hell with my family!" he shouted. "My mother..."

Maxim jotted everything down in his notepad. "Tell me about your mother?"

"No."

"Did you have any siblings?"

"One." The smuggler opened his eyes briefly—he moved in and out of consciousness. "Just one. My brother ..." His body began to convulse. His arms and legs shook. The drugs were working as intended.

"Where are you from?"

"Far away."

Maxim studied every gesture and eye movement, even the way the smuggler's lips moved. "Tell me about your brother."

"Screw you..." The smuggler's defiant voice trailed off at the end. "What's this about?"

"You should know what it's about."

"Enlighten me."

"Who hired you to deliver those weapons?"

"What weapons?"

"The chemical weapons you were delivering to the Ukrainian rebels in Ochakiv. Who hired you?"

"I won't tell you a thing."

"You will."

"I won't."

"You've been injected with a special cocktail of drugs," Maxim said. "It doesn't matter how much you fight it. You will lose. You will eventually tell me your deepest, darkest secret."

The smuggler continued to shake as he laid on the table. The brute was trying to fight off the drugs through sheer will alone.

Maxim decided to go back to his original line of questioning. He was trying to find his way into the mind of the smuggler. He knew he was close. "Who is your brother?"

"Jason," the smuggler said—his voice was strained, as if in a struggle. It was obvious that he couldn't stop himself from telling the truth.

"His last name?"

"Drake." The smuggler screamed the name, as if he was in pain.

The two Temny guards who were stood outside the interrogation room ran inside, fearing something had gone wrong. Maxim lifted up his hand as a gesture for them not to interfere with his practice.

The smuggler again tried to wiggle himself free from the confines of the table. "Get me out of this," he said.

"Who is Jason Drake?" Maxim said.

"He was a damn fool. He joined the military after I left town. The idiot."

"The US military?"

"Yes."

"Are you a member of the US military?"

"I was."

"So you don't work for the US military now?"

"Fuck you," the smuggler said.

"Colin," Maxim said, remembering the smuggler's name. "I want to help you. Do you know where you are?"

"I'm in a Ukrainian prison being interrogated by some book worm. Fuck you."

"You need to tell me who you work for. You need to tell me who hired you to deliver those weapons."

Colin's pupils were dilated. The drugs had taken over his system. He was barely in control of himself. Maxim knew he was only a couple questions away from discovering the truth, but then the unexpected happened.

Colin lifted his head and smashed it back into the table.

"What are you doing?" Maxim asked.

"I can't tell you a thing." Colin again smashed his head into the back of the table. He put all his force into it. Blood began to splatter out from the back of his head.

"Stop!" Maxim yelled. "You'll hurt yourself."

"I'll tell you nothing." Colin continued to smash his head into the part of the table that rested his head. "You should just kill me!"

"No!" Maxim said. "I can help. We can help. All you have to do is tell us—"

"Kill me! Kill me! Kill me!" Colin screamed. The blood from the back of his head had splashed onto Maxim's suit.

The Temny guards intervened. They knew the situation was getting out of control. One of them whacked Colin in the head with the butt of his rifle, rendering Colin unconscious.

Maxim stood up, looked down at the smuggler, and thought about the brief exchange. What the hell? he thought. He was so close.

He left the interrogation room.

Commander Oksi met him in the hallway. The commander had been paying close attention to the interrogation via the security cameras in the facility.

"You were close," Oksi said, a broad smile on his face. "I knew you would get something out of him."

"I got him to say his name and the name of his brother, that is all."

"It's better than my men could do. We waterboarded him, we didn't feed him for days. He wouldn't say a thing. He, at least, spoke to you."

"That's what the drugs are good for. Still, I failed. You wanted to know who hired him to deliver those weapons?"

"You will come back, yes? You will continue the interrogation?"

Maxim pushed past Oksi. "Just email me when you're ready," he said. He didn't want to be reminded about the unethical nature of everything he was doing. He was a traitor to his discipline, to his science.

Oksi laughed as Maxim stormed down the hall. "Talk soon," he yelled.

Maxim slammed the door to the stairwell and left Temny.

He wanted to be at the university. He wanted to be surrounded by his books. He wanted to help people, not leave them bloodied, tortured, and screaming to die.

ELEVEN

The fluorescent light above Sierra White's cubicle buzzed. She looked up at it and shook her head.

A headache? Again?

She closed her eyes. Maybe the dark would help.

It didn't.

While the diffused white light bothered her eyes, the sound it made was worse. It got under her skin, to the point where she couldn't concentrate.

Unlike the offices on the upper floors of the George Bush Center for Intelligence, Encrypted Comms felt like a relic of the Cold War. Large, beige cubicles separated each station. The office was located in the second-floor basement. Even the computers were old—large and loud machines rested atop each desk.

The Encrypted Comms manager quipped to Sierra during her interview that the computers were so out of date they couldn't be hacked. He thought that was a good thing.

He was an idiot, though. A company man, through and through. He'd put up with anything so long as he got his paycheck.

Sierra cracked her neck and took a deep breath. She needed to get back to work. She had a dozen more intercepted comms to analyze. It was almost the end of her shift, too.

Being an analyst in Encrypted Comms was an important job at the CIA, one that involved a special security clearance, but it was damn boring. Still, boring was what Sierra had asked for.

After all she'd been through, boring was all she could take.

There was a time when she wanted to be a field officer, but after the Langley attack and her kidnapping, she wanted nothing to do with fieldwork. She learned during that awful ordeal how far she could be pushed, how much she could take.

After her kidnapping, she was left with what her psychologist called post-traumatic stress disorder or PTSD. She couldn't sleep with the lights off. She catastrophized everything. She didn't trust anyone. She was nervous. Always. Even then, in that cubicle, her palms were wet with sweat.

She looked at the picture on her desk—the only thing that helped her calm down. Her mother, father, and she were standing in front of the red barn in Dayton, Ohio. She was fourteen when the photo was taken. She remembered how confident she felt that day.

That confidence was something she sorely missed.

She sipped a cup of tea that rested beside her phone. She needed to focus on the task at hand.

She opened up her list of comms. There were fifty tasks to complete.

An intelligence agency like the CIA received tens of thousands of intercepts each day. Encrypted Comms was the location most of those intercepts ended up. An algorithmic AI-based program siphoned through each intercept, looking for keywords. Any high-lighted intercepts would require an in-person analysis.

Sierra's job at Langley was simple. Read through intercepted communications from foreign intelligence agencies and look for anything unusual. Her analysis would be relayed to her manager, who would report on it and send it to the right unit within the CIA.

The intercepts that ended up on her desk usually concerned CIA officers out in the field; names of men and women—codenames, mostly—who were either currently running an operation or had just left one.

Most intercepts were highlighted green, which meant they were harmless. They only highlighted a foreign office, body, terror group, or intelligence agency relaying a message concerning a field operative whose identity was still hidden.

Some intercepts were black, which meant they had grisly details concerning the bodies of dead officers—fished out of the water by local law enforcement or found in the morgue of some hospital in the middle of who-knew-where. Those messages were rare.

The most important messages were red. Those were the ones that mattered most, that needed to be pushed up to the proper office.

Sierra opened up the next message in her queue.

It was black. It concerned a dead officer. It had been intercepted from a Ukrainian military complex—the Temny Facility.

It had been sent from the commanding officer at Temny to the Foreign Intelligence Service of Ukraine. The CIA carefully monitored all communication channels in the country, thanks to the conflict with Russia.

The intercept had an unusual title:

'American smuggler working for Anti-Russian forces.'

She read through the intercept.

When she read the final line, her heart skipped a beat. Had she read it correctly?

001933.20: Ukrainian Temny—clearance check.
Individual: Injured smuggler (believed). Captured during a raid at a dock on the Black Sea.
He's refused to talk during traditional or enhanced interrogation techniques. The man is trained (military?)
We brought in additional resource; Dr. Maxim Rachman.

JASON DRAKE.
Subject said his name during Dr. Rachman's interrogation. JASON DRAKE is his brother, we believe.

Subject's name: Colin.

Further interviews will be completed in the following days.

Sierra pushed herself away from her computer monitor.

JASON DRAKE.

His name was all in caps, which meant the CIA's algorithm had scanned the message and identified the name as a person of interest. She was most likely the first person to see it.

Drake was the officer who had rescued her from her kidnappers. She thought him dead. He was an ex-Terminus officer who had been recruited by the CIA Director.

Sierra printed out the message, and grabbed the paper from the printer while the ink was still warm.

Her manager called out to her before she left the office, but she ignored him.

She needed to talk to Kate Price.

TWELVE

Artem Orlov grew up in Saint Petersburg in the late eighties. His mother died from heart failure on his fifth birthday. His father tried to take care of him but did a poor job. After November 9th, 1989—the day the Berlin Wall fell—Artem's father lost his job at the steel factory.

"I am sorry, my boy," Dimitri said to his son as he packed a suitcase full of clothes. His face was damp with tears. "This is for the best."

"Papa, where are you going?" Artem asked.

"I have failed you and your mother. I promised her I would take care of you."

"Papa, I don't understand."

Dimitri finished packing his clothes and grabbed his young boy by the hand.

"You are hurting me, Papa! Where are we going?"

His father was panicked and sweating. His voice quivered when he spoke. "It will be okay, my boy." He dragged Artem down the stairwell of their apartment building and out into the blustery and cold street.

A white van stood idle in front of the building. The side doors were open, and two men in long overcoats stood on either side of it.

They were dressed like military officers. The city of Saint Petersburg was in the midst of a thick snowstorm.

"They will take care of you," Dimitri said to his son.

"Papa? What is happening?"

Dimitri knelt to the ground and wiped flakes of snow out of his eyes. He grabbed Artem by the shoulders and stared into his young child's eyes. "This is the only option, my son. This is for the best."

"What?" Artem began to cry. He was too young to understand. "Please, Papa!"

"They will take care of you."

"What do you mean? Who are they? Where am I going?"

The men standing on either side of the van's open door grabbed Artem and pulled him away from Dimitri. Artem screamed. Dimitri reached for his son's hands, but the men pushed him away—they were much taller, stronger. Dimitri fell into the snow.

Thirty years later, Artem was at a bar in a busy nightclub in Moscow. Next to him was a beautiful young woman. She listened to the story about his past, enthralled by the tragedy.

"That was more thirty years ago," Artem said. He looked at his glass of vodka. It glowed thanks to the red laser lights that crossed along the dance floor of the club.

"Your father sold you?" the woman asked.

Artem shot back the glass of vodka. "No," he said. "He gave me away. He handed me over to the military. He showed them my test scores from school—math and science. They seemed convinced that I was a worthy investment. Apparently, it happened all the time in the days of the USSR. I was one of the last handed over to the government."

"Why did he do that?"

"Because he knew he couldn't care for me. He knew it was the best shot I had at a long life. You have to remember, no one in Russia knew what was going to happen after the wall fell. When the jobs started to disappear, people panicked. You're too young to remember."

Artem felt her touch. Her hand felt nice as it stroked along his back; it crawled up his spine.

He looked at her. She had short hair that was dyed blue. Her makeup exaggerated her eyes, and her skirt was far too short.

"He did what was best for you," she said. "He wanted a better life for you."

"He did what he had to do."

"And what about your father now?"

"He's dead," Artem said.

The woman turned away.

"Just remember that life in Russia in the nineties, after the fall, was no picnic," Artem said. "Many found the transition from Communist to Democratic rule difficult—even if, at the end of the day, it was all just a show. The oligarchs, the ones truly in power, simply changed their clothes and titles. The only thing that truly changed in Russia was the arrival of McDonald's hamburgers and Nike shoes."

"I'm sorry," she said.

"Enough about my past," he said. "I want to have fun. I have had a busy week."

"Of course," the young woman said. "I'm sorry for asking about your youth. You just had a look of sadness in your eyes. I had to inquire. It's my nature."

Artem half-smiled. It wasn't the first time someone had accused him of having sad eyes. "You ask good questions," he said. "What do you do for a living?"

"I'm a reporter," she said. "I write for a foreign paper."

"Which one?"

"I can't tell you," she said. "It could get me killed."

"What do you report on?"

"Russian politics."

Artem ordered another shot of vodka and quickly tossed it back. "Do you want to dance?" he asked.

She smiled.

He followed the young reporter onto the dance floor. Once there, he stared into her eyes—into the beauty of her youth. She turned away nervously, blushing. He made her feel uncomfortable but intrigued.

Artem pulled the woman in close. It was forceful, almost violent.

She stared up at him and quivered. "Are you okay?" she asked, fearful of his sudden aggression.

"I don't want to dance," he said. "Take me to your apartment."

"I ..."

He kissed her.

She pushed him away. "I don't usually like fast men," she said.

"I'm sorry," he said. "I just want to talk. You listen. So many ignore me."

She smiled and rested her head on his chest. She could feel his heartbeat. She'd taken the bait. "Okay," she said.

Artem took her by the hand, and the two of them pushed through the thick crowd of drunken revelers. They made their way outside onto the street. It was raining and dark. The streetlights flickered, and a neon green light atop a pharmacy on the other side of the street lit up the puddles with reflected light.

The bouncer outside the club nodded at Artem. "Mr. Orlov," the bouncer said. "It's good to see you."

Artem nodded.

The young reporter was still holding Artem's hand. He pulled her in close and said to her, "Where do you live?"

She blushed. "I haven't even told you my name," she said.

"Well, what is it?"

"It's Sashina."

"Of course it is. Where do you live, Sashina?"

She looked into his eyes nervously and didn't respond.

"I'm waiting for an answer," he said.

"Okay," Sashina said. "You can come home with me."

Artem kissed her. This time, she didn't push him away. She accepted it.

After their kiss, he let her go.

Sashina hailed for a cab. They both got inside.

Artem checked his phone. He'd missed three calls. Three calls from his place of work.

As the cab drove them to her apartment, Artem called the number. The person on the other end picked up immediately.

"What is it?" Artem asked.

"It's about a job," the person on the other end said.

"I am in the middle of one right now. Can't this wait?"

"No."

"What's it about?"

"A man is being held in a facility in Ukraine. The Temny Facility. You need to kill him before he talks. This is priority."

Artem looked at Sashina and smiled. She was staring out the window of the cab.

"Are you alone?" the person on the other end asked.

"I'm enjoying a night out with a beautiful lady," Artem said.

"Are you torturing her?"

Artem chuckled.

"Why are you laughing? I know your style."

"Can this wait?"

"Kill her and get to Kyiv. This is priority. Straight from the top."

"Okay," Artem said.

"It'll be worth your while."

"Goodbye." Artem hung up.

"Who was that?" Sashina asked.

"Oh, just my boss. He has some work for me."

"What do you do?"

"I'll tell you at your apartment."

THIRTEEN

Sierra took an elevator up three floors to the CIA Director's office. She felt uneasy as she stood beside her colleagues in the elevator. Personnel within the agency seemed paranoid, more so than usual. Everyone seemed uptight, nervous.

She stepped out of the elevator and walked through the halls toward the director's office.

Groups of officers and analysts were huddled in the corners. Everyone glanced at each other suspiciously.

Something was going down. Something big. A coup? Why hadn't she heard anything? Was there something she didn't know about, she thought.

Life in DC had grown more political recently. Maybe it was because it was an election year—one man backed corporate interests against another man backed by corporate interests. Two factions warring with each other, trying to convince the public that they were different. Had CIA personnel picked its side? Were battle lines being drawn?

The body politic in an organization like Langley was more akin to a reality television show than anything else.

She ignored the looks on the faces of fellow CIA personnel and

walked down the long quiet corridor toward Price's office. The director's receptionist acknowledged her as she approached.

"Is she in?" Sierra asked the receptionist.

"She just got in, but I don't—"

Sierra ignored her and barged into Price's office. She slammed
the door behind her.

Price was at her desk. "I was about to call you," Price said.

"You were?"

"I've been fired," Price said.

"What? Why?" Sierra asked.

Price looked around her office and shook her head. "It doesn't
matter," she said. "It's bullshit."

"Read this!" Sierra said. She slammed the printed intercept on
Price's desk.

Price looked at the paper. She then looked up at Sierra. "What's
this about?"

"This concerns an operation in Ukraine," Sierra said. "Ukrainian
special forces just apprehended a man they believe to be a smuggler.
He's being held in a military facility in Kyiv."

"President Clarkson won't approve of any operation in Ukraine.
He's scared to make a move. He's more worried about his public
image than he is about Russia and world order. That's why I've been
fired. I told him we need to intervene. He disagreed."

"Read the intercept," Sierra said. "It concerns Jason."

Price picked up the paper. She read through it. Her skin turned
white. "I need a drink," she said.

"We need to question this guy," Sierra said. "Who is he? The
Ukrainians say his name is Colin. He said he's Jason's brother? Do
you know anything about this? Did Jason have a brother?"

Price walked to her liquor cabinet and pulled out a bottle of
vodka. She poured herself a glass and shot it back.

"What should we do?" Sierra asked.

"We do nothing," Price said. "It's like I said, Clarkson wants us to
keep our cool. We can't get involved. If we do, we'll end up in prison."

"You always said to bring anything about Jason to you. I figured that's why you put me in Encrypted Comms. Do you know who Colin is?"

"I put you in comms because you wanted something boring," Price said. "Jason is dead ... isn't he?"

"All the intel we gathered confirmed as much. The Russians killed him when they destroyed the military facility in Gerdansk—no survivors were found in the facility."

"I survived," Price said. "And so did a couple of others ..." Her voice drifted off, and she poured herself another drink.

"Then what should we do?"

"Every move I make is being monitored. I'm sure you've felt the paranoia in the hallways. Word spreads quickly, doesn't it? I can feel the vultures circling my body. Every analyst, executive, and director worried about their career knows they should stay miles away from me. I have no one I can rely on."

"You can rely on me."

"We believe Jason is dead."

"Yes," Sierra said. "We've already gone over that."

"But, as far as I knew, I thought Colin was dead, too."

"What do you mean?"

"Jason's brother—I knew a little about him. Jason told me about him during his Terminus assessment. When I pressed Jason about his brother, he shrugged. All he told me was that his brother was a soldier in the army and was killed in Iraq. He said he hardly knew his brother."

"So, you think this intercept is bogus?"

"No," Price said. "It's unusual. It might be unlikely. But at the very least, we should investigate."

"So, you'll send an officer into Kyiv? You'll find out what the Ukrainian military knows?"

"I can't," Price said. "No director or station chief will accept the mission and, even if they do, word will get to the President. Whatever I do needs to be off the books. It needs to be between you and me. Understand?"

Sierra looked at Price. She clenched her jaw and felt her heart rate elevate. Was she having another panic attack?

"Are you okay?" Price asked.

"I'm fine," Sierra said. "I don't know what you're asking. Can you be clear?"

"You need to head to Ukraine," Price said. "You need to get to the bottom of this."

"I don't want any action. I want to stay here."

"It'll be a fact-finding mission," Price said. "All you need to do is head to Kyiv, speak to the officials who are holding the prisoner, and determine if there's any validity to the subject's claim. If he is Jason's brother, then we should find out what we can. After all, he was an ex-American soldier. How did he fake his death? Why is he working for Ukrainian rebels? We need to get to the bottom of it. If there is a kernel of truth to any of this, perhaps we can use it to get the President to act."

"But—"

"You'll be okay," Price said. "You spent years in the office, running names, reading transcripts or receipts. You've come to terms that the life of a CIA officer is more paperwork than action. Field-work is similar—it's not nearly as exciting as you think it is. I spent twenty years in the field. Ten as an officer, ten as a station chief. It was boring work. Use the intel from that manuscript to get in contact with the university professor who interrogated the smuggler. Maybe he can arrange a meeting with you, or at least share what he knows. You have to go alone. You have to keep this as quiet as you can."

Sierra nodded but did not fully grasp it all. Ten minutes ago, she had been complaining about how tedious her job was. Now she was terrified her job was going to kill her. "I really don't think I'm ready for this," Sierra said. "I can't—"

Price turned away and looked out over the trees in Langley Oaks Park outside her window. "You're right," she said. "You shouldn't do this alone. You'll need help."

"You just told me I'm the only one here you can trust."

"When Jason was in the South Dakota, he grew close to a woman. I've had eyes on her. She's been busy the last few months. I suspect she knows something."

"You think Jason is alive?"

"I don't know."

"So, before I head to Kyiv ... I should try to track down Jason."

"Maybe," Price said. "I don't know."

"Where is the woman? Where in South Dakota?"

"She works at a bar called The Hunter's Lodge. It's in a town called Deadwood."

"And if she knows nothing about Jason?"

"Then you go to Kyiv alone."

"But—"

"You can do this, Sierra—I know you can. Trust your gut."

Sierra closed her eyes. She took a deep breath and left Price's office, unsure what had just happened. Whatever it was, she knew her life was about to change.

FOURTEEN

An empty glass sat atop the bar of the Hunter's Lodge. It'd just been placed there by a man in a leather jacket. It glistened in the dark light of the bar. Hank Williams's 'I'm So Lonesome I Could Cry' echoed throughout the warm and dusty bar. The sounds of the song pulsated from the tinny speakers of the jukebox. The somber and sad tone of Williams's voice soothed the rough, weathered faces of those drinking inside the bar.

Ruby Claire grabbed the glass from the bar. It was five minutes to last call, and she was behind schedule. She placed the glass into the sink and turned back to the sad drunks, buffoons, and locals who visited her bar nightly.

"Can't I have another," Phill Delaney said to her. He was about ten past drunk. The fact that he still could put together a cohesive sentence surprised Ruby.

She'd cut Phill off hours ago. He'd refused to leave.

"You're done, Phill," Ruby said, smiling. "You need to slow down, old man. You're not the young buck you used to be."

Phill's face turned sour. He tried to stand up from his stool but stumbled backward. A couple of mountain bikers who were traveling through town caught him before he fell. They helped Phill back onto his seat.

"Now, you listen here, young—" Phill belched. "You listen here, young lady. I am ... I don't take kindly to those words. You think I'm drunk?"

"You are, Phill."

He belched again. "I am not!"

He stood up again but, like before, lost his balance. The mountain bikers weren't as aware this time. Phill fell on his ass.

Ruby rolled her eyes. She nodded at the bouncer who was stood at the door and went back to her tasks—glasses, plates, and coasters needed to be cleaned up. She needed to wipe down the counters. She looked at the clock. It was almost two a.m. She had to get home.

The bouncer helped Phill up and escorted him out. Phill didn't fight it. He was too drunk to know what was going on.

Hank Williams's song came to an end and Ruby seized advantage of the silence. "Get out!" she shouted. "We're closing up!"

The locals got up from their seats, and those traveling through town followed suit. They made their way out into the dark. All of them seemed sullen, defeated. A small town like Deadwood wasn't exactly the most optimistic place in America.

Ruby finished up her tasks as quickly as she could and grabbed her coat from the rack.

The bouncer held the door open for her as she went outside. "You need a smoke?" he asked.

The bouncer's name was Chuck. He was a good guy. Simple-minded, but loyal—and strong as a horse. As long as you didn't badmouth Batman comics, he was a gentle giant. Chuck liked his superheroes—especially DC ones.

"I'm fine, Chuck," she said. "I need to check on the dog. He needs his medicine. He's sick."

"Really?"

"Yes."

Chuck gave Ruby a concerned look and nodded at her.

Ruby walked down the lonesome downtown street of Deadwood. The wind howled, and the street lights flickered. She walked past O'Malley's Diner and Wayne's Auto. The fact that it was mid-summer meant the town was busier than usual. The town wasn't very popular during the winter months. The ski hills in the area were too dangerous, and the town itself was considered too remote, but the summer brought in the hikers and adventure-seeking individuals.

Her apartment was above 2Cuts Barbershop. She walked up the iron fire escape at the back of the building and unlocked the front door to her apartment.

Houston, the Bedouin sheepdog she'd inherited from Drake, was curled up on the couch. The dog's eyes opened slowly as she walked inside.

"Don't!" Ruby said, dropping her purse and running to the dog.

Houston didn't listen to her. He grunted and stood up. His legs wobbled, and he almost fell off of the couch.

Ruby met the animal before he fell. She held the dog close. "You old fool," she said, stroking the animal's neck and pulling it in close. "You're too damn stubborn."

The dog closed its eyes and rested his head against her chest.

"He'll come back soon," she said. "I know he will. I sent him everything he asked for. I gave him what he wanted. He said two weeks—maybe three. He'll be here—and then we can leave."

The old dog collapsed in her lap.

Ruby shook her head. The animal was so much like the man who owned him that it almost made her laugh. The vet had said Houston should have been dead months ago. The old dog just refused to quit.

Ruby had only known Drake for a short time, but long enough that she knew that he would stop at nothing once he made up his mind. Like Houston, he was a survivor, a fighter.

She comforted Houston for a couple more minutes and then, satisfied that the dog was at ease, stood up from the couch and walked to her computer.

She needed to check her email.

He was supposed to respond.

FIFTEEN

Six months ago, Ruby received an email from an anonymous account. The subject of the email made her heart skip a beat: 'My dog.' Despite feeling nervous, she'd opened the message.

Ruby,
I need help.
How's Houston?
- J

It was him.

She had believed he was dead. The whole world thought he was dead. After all, he was the man who'd been accused of attacking the President—the man who the FBI had apprehended after the attack on the capital. He was an enemy of the state.

He was also the man who'd saved her life.

Drake had come to Deadwood months before all the shit hit the fan. He'd kept to himself mostly—he had a cabin out in the woods and came into town only for supplies or to watch the hockey game at the bar—he liked the NHL club the Dallas Stars.

That was where Ruby first saw him.

"What do you want?" she'd asked.

He sat behind the bar and barely seemed to notice her. His eyes seemed to scan the room—they darted from left to right. It was almost as if he was taking a picture of everyone's face and recording it to memory.

"Beer," he said.

"We have a lot of beer," she said. "Budweiser, Coors, Molson—"

"Molson."

She grabbed him his drink.

"Thanks," he grunted.

What struck Ruby as odd during their first meeting was that he hardly paid attention to her. It wasn't that he hadn't looked at her, but that he seemed ready to move at a moment's notice.

"You okay?" she asked.

"Yes," he said.

"You seem on edge."

He smiled. "I just want to drink."

"Where are you from?"

"Texas."

"And what brings you here?"

"Work."

"What kind of work?"

"Hunting."

She took an immediate liking to him. There was something about his eyes that told her he was kind, that he wasn't a threat. Still, there was a darkness in him. Something sinister—something dangerous.

After that first meeting, they became very close. They'd spend nights in his cabin.

"Tell me about your past," she said. "You hardly talk about yourself."

"There isn't much to say."

The two of them sat on his bed in his cabin. He had his arms around her. The fire from his wood stove burned bright.

"I've told you everything about me."

"You volunteered that information," he said, a wry smile on his face.

She looked at his broad face and gave him a mean look. "You're strange, you know that?"

"I know," he said.

"You can't tell me anything? I've been seeing you for weeks, and all I know is that you're a damn good hunter, and you like the Dallas Stars."

"There isn't much more to me."

"There isn't?"

"No."

"That's a lie," she said. She pushed herself from his arms and stood up. "I have every reason to leave."

"Then go."

"Ah, fuck you," she said. "You're just another stranger rolling through town. Are you a criminal? Are you an ex-con?"

Ruby put her clothes back on. Drake rubbed his hand through his hair and sat up in the bed. "Calm down," he said.

The two of them became close. They told each other their deepest secrets and fears.

But that moment was short-lived. Everything went to shit when one of his old CIA buddies came looking for him. Ruby took a bullet in her stomach as a result. Drake said he had to go. All that Ruby had in memory of him was his dog. Houston couldn't go with him.

It wasn't until she saw his face on television after President Clarkson had been shot during his inauguration that she had any idea how messed up his past was.

He was an assassin, one trained by the CIA.

As the months past, she figured he was dead.

There was no way he'd leave his dog behind, she'd thought.

But then, she received his message.

How's Houston?

He was alive.

She carefully responded to the message.

Who is this?

She didn't send anything else. A part of her didn't want it to be him—although she'd be lying if she said that was the larger part.

A day later, she got a response.

You have a tattoo on your left ankle. It's of a feather. I kissed it the first night we made love.

It's me.

Over the next month, they communicated back and forth. His messages were short, nondescript. He didn't give anything away. He seemed to be testing her. He obviously wanted to make sure she hadn't informed any government official about their communications.

The first few emails concerned mostly Houston's wellbeing.

The last one she received was more of a warning.

It won't be long before they come for you.

Ruby was a small-town girl from South Dakota. She didn't want trouble. She wanted to know what Drake meant by *they*.

What are you talking about?"

His response was clear:

You know who I am talking about. You have my dog. I doubt they think I am dead. It won't be long before you're brought in. They will break you. They will threaten you. You need to be careful.

Help me and I can help you.

The '*they*' was the CIA, Drake's former employer, that much was clear. Drake had reached out to her because he cared about her—and the dog. He wanted them safe. He didn't trust the CIA. He considered them an enemy.

She agreed to help him. She didn't know why. Maybe it was

because she was done with her job ... maybe it was something else. In any case, she did what he'd asked her to do.

She took two weeks off work and drove, with Houston in the back seat of her hatchback, to Thunder Bay, Ontario. Drake had a contact there. A man named Vincent—a former Canadian CSIS officer.

She got everything Drake needed; paperwork, documentation, and money. Vincent was an old ally. He'd run operations with Drake in Afghanistan. "Bad ones," Vincent said. "Very bad." All he said to Sierra after her handing the documents and money was to "Be careful." She didn't respond. She just took what he gave her and sent it to Drake.

That all happened a month ago.

Since then, she'd spent every night checking her email, waiting for a response, waiting for confirmation that he got it all. He told her once he had the passports he'd be able to head back to Deadwood. He just needed the paperwork.

There were no new messages in her inbox.

She closed her eyes.

Would she hear from her again? Had he played her? The thoughts did drift through her head. Still, she had Houston and she knew that Drake wouldn't leave him alone.

She scratched the dog under the chin, stood up, and walked to her bedroom. She had an early morning. She was opening the Hunter's Lodge.

SIXTEEN

Sierra opened her suitcase. She didn't know how long she'd be gone. She didn't really care. Since leaving Price's office, she hadn't really thought too much about anything. She left Langley, went home, had a glass of wine, and began to pack.

The Hunter's Lodge?

Ruby?

Her mind raced.

What the hell was she doing?

She called Price after stuffing an expensive blouse into her luggage. "What is this?" she asked. "Everything is happening too quickly. I should have asked more questions when I was in your office."

"Don't be scared," Price said on the other end.

"Don't be scared? Why do you think Jason is alive? What's going on? I just wanted to share with you an intercept from Ukraine."

"I already told you. I don't know if Jason's dead. All we have is a Russian report that everyone who was in Gerdansk died. That's it."

"And what's this bar, the Hunter's Lodge, have to do with anything?"

"Just go there and ask for Ruby."

"Who is she?"

Price sighed. "It will be okay, Sierra. You have to trust me."

Sierra stared at her suitcase. She'd packed too much. That was something she always did. She felt childish. Stupid, like she didn't know what she was doing. "Okay," she said.

"Good," Price said. "If you go to Ukraine and Jason's brother is alive, you'll wish you had Jason at your side. You know that."

"This seems desperate."

"Well, you're not a field officer. I am desperate. And, I'm willing to bet that Jason is alive. If I'm wrong ... well, my career is over anyway. And, truthfully, I don't give a shit about that. I just want the President to do the right thing. Frankly, we need every bit of help we can get."

"And if this Ruby knows nothing? If she doesn't know anything about Jason?"

"Then you head to Ukraine and we hope for a miracle. You talk to the Professor who wrote the intercept. You investigate."

"You know I can't do that," Sierra said. "I'm not ready."

"That's why you need to look for Jason first." Price hung up. Either the conversation was starting to bug her or someone had come into her office.

In any case, Sierra didn't mind. She finished packing her clothes and then made her way to the Dulles International Airport.

As she sat at the terminal, watching a handler on the tarmac load some baggage into a Boeing 777 aircraft, she thought about her brief encounters with Drake.

The first time she met him was at Dulles. He'd just stepped off of a private jet that had been flown from a Royal Air Force airfield in England. He had walked with a strange sense of confidence and swagger. Her beauty hadn't intimidated him. That had made her nervous.

Sierra's mind wavered as she boarded the flight to South Dakota in the afternoon.

Was she jealous of Ruby? She wasn't sure.

She closed her eyes and tried not to think of anything but the fact that for first time since joining the CIA she'd been given her own assignment—even if was completely confidential and associated with

Kate Price, about as toxic an individual as one could find in all of DC by that point.

As the tires skidded against the tarmac in South Dakota, Sierra woke up. She grabbed her things, hailed for a cab, and told the cabbie to take her to Deadwood and the Hunter's Lodge.

"You got it, lady," the cabbie said.

She sat in the back of the cab and told herself that Price was actually looking out for her by sending her to South Dakota. She wanted Sierra to have all the help she could get. Although, deep down, Sierra doubted Price's intentions.

"No," she whispered to herself. "Don't think that way."

The cabbie looked back at her through the rearview mirror. "You okay, miss?"

"I'm fine," Sierra said. "I'll be fine."

SEVENTEEN

It was another rowdy night at The Hunter's Lodge. Ruby was glad it was busy. She didn't have time to think about Drake—to worry about why hadn't he emailed.

As she filled out up a pint for Phill, who was already well on his way to being too drunk again, she noticed, in the corner of her eye, a woman walk in to the bar. She definitely wasn't a local.

Ruby kept her eye on the new guest. There was something about her that made her alarm bells ring. Whether it was the Gucci handbag or the stilettos, it was clear that the woman didn't belong in Deadwood.

The new arrival sat down at the bar. She looked nervous and scared. Her eyes darted left and right, like she was looking for someone.

"You want a drink?" Ruby asked. She leered down at the woman from behind the bar. Whoever she was, she was attractive—too attractive. The men in the bar were finding it difficult not to look at her and the women were getting upset.

"Glass of red," the woman said.

Ruby smirked. "Where are you from, sweetheart?"

"DC."

"And what's someone from DC doing in a small, shit hole like Deadwood on a Wednesday night?"

"I'm looking for someone."

"Who?"

"Someone named Ruby Claire."

Phill laughed. He'd been eavesdropping the whole time. He still wasn't drunk enough to be lost in his own mind, in his pain and regret. "Well, you found her sweetheart. You're talking to Ruby."

Ruby's eyes narrowed and she shot Phill an angry glance. She wanted go wring his neck.

"You're Ruby Claire?" the woman at the bar asked.

Ruby turned back to her and nodded. She tried to be cool, collected. "Who wants to know?"

"My name is Sierra White."

"Why are you here and what do you want with me?"

"A man used to live in this town. His name was Jason Drake. I'm from ..." She paused. "I used to work with him."

Ruby's fists clenched. Her pulse pounded. She had the urge to flee. "I don't know what you're talking about," Ruby said in a slow and specific way. She wanted to make it clear to the woman at the bar that she was done with the conversation.

"I know you're lying," Sierra said. "I'm not here to scare you. I'm just looking for him."

"I already told you. I don't know a thing."

"The Director of the CIA sent me here. Her name's Kate Price. She said you were close with Jason."

Phill was still eavesdropping. While he wasn't drunk enough to not follow the conversation, he was drunk enough to not pick up on Ruby's cues. He opened his big mouth. "Jason? That name sounds familiar. Ruby, didn't you know someone? The big guy. He lived out in the woods, right? He used to come by here and watch the hockey games. Guy was a real weirdo. He disappeared after the sheriff died."

Ruby gritted her teeth. There was no point in fighting it now. She closed her eyes and tried to think of something to say.

"I know why you want to deny knowing him," Sierra said. "But you need to understand that I am a friend. I want to help. I can help."

"He warned me that you might show up again. I'm sure you know he's dead."

"Is he?"

"Is that why you're here?"

"Is there a more private place we can talk?"

"My shift ends in an hour. Meet me outside."

Sierra stood up and left the bar.

EIGHTEEN

Sierra wasn't just nervous. She was downright terrified. She stood out in the parking lot outside of the bar and waited for Ruby. It was one AM and colder than she thought it would be. She'd never been to South Dakota in the summer. It felt like DC in the fall. She should have packed a sweater.

As patrons slowly crept out of the bar, all in various states of sobriety, she held her breath. Was she stupid trusting Ruby? Would she run? What was she even doing?

And then the lights in the bar turned off. Ruby walked out the front doors, nodded at the bouncer, and approached Sierra.

"Follow me," Ruby said.

Sierra followed Ruby to her apartment. She didn't say a thing.

Ruby opened her apartment door, Sierra felt more nervous. Something was wrong.

"Go ahead," Ruby said.

Sierra walked inside. She then stopped. She felt something at the back of her head. She stood on a doormat. Her legs shook. She wasn't ready for this.

"Are you going to kill me?"

"Who are you?" Ruby asked. "Tell me or I'll shoot you in the head. I have lots of friends in this town."

Sierra nodded. "I figured that was a pistol you had against my head. It's not the first time someone has pointed a gun at me point blank."

"Who sent you?"

"You already know," Sierra said. "Or you would have killed me."

Ruby smiled. "You're smarter than you look."

Lying on the couch, in his usual spot, Houston spotted the action at the door. The old dog stood up, his legs shaking. He made his way to the doorway.

"Houston!" Sierra said. "You have his dog?"

Ruby nodded, shocked to hear that Sierra had known Drake that well. "So, you did know Jason, eh?"

The dog walked up to Sierra. His tail wagged the whole way from the couch. Sierra knelt to the ground and scratched the old-looking dog behind his ears. She forgot that a gun had just been pointed at her head. "I met Houston a couple years back. It was just after Jason had come back to the country."

"If Houston didn't know you, I was going to ..." Ruby didn't finish sentence. She put the pistol behind her belt.

Sierra looked up at her. She got the hint. Houston was a way for Ruby to measure someones trust. She'd passed the test. "Is he alive?"

"Jason is dead."

"My boss doesn't think so."

"Kate Price?"

"You know her?"

"Yes," Ruby said. "A little while ago, Kate Price showed up here and I ended up getting shot." She lifted up her shirt revealing the wound on her stomach.

"So, you know he was CIA?"

"I know what I need to know about him. He told me little. Most likely, in an attempt to protect me, but clearly that didn't work. He left with Kate after I was shot. He left me his dog. I didn't hear from him. So, I figured he was dead." Tears began to fall from her eyes.

Sierra stood up and put her arm on Ruby's shoulder. "I'm sorry for wasting your time. I came here because Kate has eyes on you. She's like that. She's paranoid. All the time. She figured if Jason was alive, he'd reach out to you. And now ..." She gestured to Houston. "Now, I know why. Jason loved his dog. But if you say he's dead, then he's dead."

Ruby sensed that there was a sincerity behind Sierra's eyes. "What is this about?"

"I might as well tell you," Sierra said. "My whole career is tied to Kate and she's, well ... She's not someone you want to be associated with at Langley right now. Needless to say, I figured this would be a false errand. No one could have survived the attack on Gerdansk. No one. Not even Jason."

"Do you want a coffee or something?" Ruby asked.

"It's late," Sierra said. "I have a hotel room booked on the other side of town and I just need to sleep. I have to head to Ukraine in the morning."

"Ukraine?"

"Yes."

"What's in Ukraine that concerns Jason?"

"Does it matter?" Sierra asked. "He's dead. I came here out of some false hope. Everything at Langley that he fought to protect has turned to shit. It's all coming apart." Sierra walked to the door and opened it. "Thank you for your help."

Ruby looked at Houston and then back at Sierra. "Houston really likes you."

"I'm surprised the old dog is still kicking," Sierra said, a warm smile on her face.

"He's like Jason. He doesn't give up."

"Or Jason was like him."

"No," Ruby said.

Sierra tensed up. The panic that had subsided after seeing the dog had come back. "What do you mean?" she asked. Her mouth felt dry.

"I shouldn't ... I am ... I am scared."

"So am I."

"I know," Ruby said. "Jason told me never trust you guys, but I haven't heard from him and you seem genuine, real."

"Is he alive?"

"Yes," Ruby said. "He's alive."

NINETEEN

The sun rose, and the sand shimmered. Covered in a thick sweat, Drake dove into the sea and let the thoughts of his past wash away. His mind had been adrift in regret and pain since the dream of his brother.

As he dove under sparkling blue water, he closed his eyes. He surfaced and took a deep breath. Feeling refreshed, he left the water and made his way toward his cabin.

He'd been running for hours along the beach. During that time, he'd come to a conclusion: there was no escaping his past. He'd have to go home and get to the bottom of it all.

As he walked back to his cabin, he spotted a woman in a red bikini eyeing him up on the beach. She was beside a young man who was probably her fiancé. He was busy looking at his phone and had a soft belly.

Drake winked at the girl.

She blushed, turned away, and picked up a magazine.

Drake chuckled and walked up the steps of the veranda that surrounded his cabin. A lizard crawled up the front door. He waited for the tiny animal to jump off before opening his door and walking inside.

His cabin was spare and mostly empty. He liked to travel light. If he had to run, if he had to disappear, he wanted to be able to leave at a moment's notice without leaving a trace.

After showering, he got dressed. He put on a pair of khakis and a t-shirt. He then grabbed his backpack and sunglasses. He stuffed the money and passport Ruby had sent him into his back pocket. He figured he'd head to town, get a coffee, and visit an internet cafe to update her that he'd received the goods.

He left his cabin and made his way to the beach, toward the footpath that would take him into town. As he walked, he spotted Pok. The kid looked nervous, upset. Pok ran up to him at a full sprint.

"What is it?" Drake said, grabbing the boy by the shoulders. The kid was unusually panicked.

"The police," Pok said, partially out of breath. "They're looking for you."

"What? What do you mean?"

"I heard them when I was walking by the station this morning. They know you're here. They don't know your name, but the man they're looking for is you."

"How do you know?"

"They were holding a photo of you," Pok said. "I snagged it from them." Pok handed Drake the photo. Drake looked at it. It was his CIA headshot—the one that had adorned his ID card for years.

"Is something wrong?" Pok said. "Can I help? I have an uncle in India. You can—"

"You need to leave, kid," Drake grunted.

"What?"

"You need to pretend you never saw me. If anyone asks, play dumb."

Pok looked at Drake, confused. "What do you mean? I don't understand."

Drake hated to be mean to the kid, but he had to do what he had to do. "You need to go," he said. "Whoever is looking for me ... they'll not play nice."

"But ..."

"You're a smart kid, and you need to be real smart right now. You need to stay low. Forget me. I'm not someone you want to be close to."

Pok wiped tears from his eyes. "Will you come back?"

"No," Drake said, standing up. "Remember what I told you, kid. You're better than you think you are. You're better than men like me."

Drake looked up and down the street. The coast was clear for now.

No cops.

"Wait!" Pok said.

Drake ignored the kid's cries. He walked into the thick of the crowd and disappeared.

TWENTY

Artem looked down at the body of the reporter. She was nude, her limbs sprawled out on her wide and lush bed. She had died in an almost graceful pose—like an angel in a Renaissance painting or a ballerina in mid-leap. Her legs were slightly spread, her face emotionless, and her arms were sprawled out like wings.

He'd had fun with her before he'd killed her. He couldn't resist himself.

She had been foolish to trust him. And now, her youthful face was forever frozen in its current shape. At least, until her body decomposed. He'd rescued her from the cruelty of growing old, he thought.

She lived on the thirty-sixth floor of a ritzy condo in the middle of Moscow. A child of privilege. She'd thought she was an activist. She'd thought her wealth and connections would protect her. She'd thought that her public platform would protect her.

She was wrong.

Her articles about the Russian President had made her a target. She needed to be silenced. She was asking too many questions and upsetting the balance of power.

Artem got dressed and walked out of the reporter's condo. He wasn't worried about security cameras or police. He knew that the men who'd hired him would have already paid them off.

He walked through the streets of Moscow as a light rain fell.

He made his way to a bar called The Mendelev, which was only a thirty-minute walk from the reporter's condo.

If Paris was the City of Light, Moscow was the City of Rats. Since the fall of the Soviet Union, underground gangs and organized crime syndicates had found a way to run supreme. The Mendelev was a home in the underworld. It was there that Artem felt the most at ease.

The story he'd told the reporter about his youth, about his father selling him to military officials before the fall of the wall, was true. He'd just left out the part about what had happened after the wall fell.

It was bad.

The military facility that'd taken him in had fallen apart. One of the officers at the facility, needing work, became a hitman for the mafia. He'd brought the twelve-year-old Artem along with him to act as his protege.

Artem killed his first man at the age of fifteen while working on a job with the former military officer turned hitman.

He moved his way up through the underworld.

It wasn't until his mid-thirties, after working as a hitman for a group that called themselves the Company, that he felt a sense of control over his life. They gave him what he wanted, which was comfort and peace. All he had to do was kill whoever they told him to kill.

After a drink at The Mendelev, he left the bar and made his way to the Leningradsky train station. The Company had another job for him, which meant that they'd already placed everything he'd need for it in a safety deposit box that was rented in his name at the station.

He walked to the locker box and opened it up. Passports, cash, schematics for a Ukrainian facility, a plane ticket, and a box full of photographs.

He stuffed it all into his backpack and left the train station.

He had his next target, and he had everything he'd need to get the job done.

TWENTY-ONE

There was no escape. His face had been plastered up on the walls of every building in the village. Local shop owners gave him weary looks as he ran past. If they could come after him in a small place like Sansor, they could come after him anywhere.

He kept his head low and moved carefully. He only stopped when he saw a police patrol. Royal Thai Police officers moved in groups of five or six, up and down the narrow streets holding batons. He knew they were looking for him.

As he moved through Sansor, a part of him thought about disappearing into the mountains surrounding Phuket and waiting until the police gave up their search. But if Drake was sure of one thing, it was that whoever wanted him, wanted to talk—nothing more. There were two reasons that led him to that conclusion: one was the picture they used, the other was the crime they accused him of.

First, the picture they were using to identify him was taken during one of his first days as a CIA officer for Terminus. The search warrant had come from Langley—someone high up.

Second, the crime he was wanted for was thievery. A crime that meant he'd be easily extradited back to the US if caught.

Something had gone wrong back home. He worried about Ruby. He couldn't let them hurt her. She'd risked so much for him. So instead of running and hiding, he made his way to the Sansor police station. He'd meet the bull head-on.

Thirty minutes after chatting with Pok on the outskirts of the beach, he stood across from the police station. The station was four stories tall. A mangle of electrical wires and power transformers were hung up on a hydro pole just outside the building.

He crossed the street and made his way into the station.

Inside, the air was thick. The receptionist had a rotating fan on her desk. Her eyes widened when she saw him.

He approached her, leaned on her desk, and looked around the lobby. It was mostly empty. "How's it going?"

"You're the man, the man on the poster—"

Others in the police station noticed Drake—his face, his scar. It was definitely the guy on the poster.

Drake lifted his hands into the air. He could sense the tension. This was what he wanted.

"Don't move!" he heard a cop say in a thick Thai accent. "Stand down!"

Drake glanced behind him. The young cop looked like he would have weighed 130 pounds soaking wet.

"I'm not going to move," Drake said. "I'm giving myself up. You can relax."

"Don't move!" the cop shouted.

"Are those the only English words you know?"

"Shut up," the Thai cop said nervously.

The cop was close. Drake could smell the breakfast on his breath.

Due to the fact that there are no standard-issue firearms in the Royal Thai Police, Drake figured the cop threatening him wasn't carrying a firearm. If a cop in Thailand wanted a firearm, they had to pay for it themself.

Drake turned around, his arms still raised. He did it slowly.

The action made the young cop jump. He swung the baton he was holding at Drake.

Drake caught the baton and twisted it so the young cop's frail wrist bent out of shape. He heard a snap.

The cop howled and fell to his knees.

In his periphery, Drake saw more cops running into the small foyer from another room. A couple of them were holding guns. He raised his hands again and put them behind his head. He dropped to his knees beside the young cop who was writhing.

A group of officers surrounded him, yelling at him in a mixture of bad English and Thai. He was whacked in the back of the head.

"For fuck's sake," he yelled, more annoyed than in pain.

"Okay, okay," a voice said from behind the group of cops. "Step aside, fellas." A small man in a tight-fitting uniform walked toward Drake. He was the Chief Officer. He looked no taller than five-foot-five, and he had a haircut that belonged in a seventies cop show. "Bring him to my office. He's the man we're looking for."

Drake smiled. He wasn't being arrested. He was being taken to the Chief Officer's office.

"Follow me," the short man said to Drake as he stood up. "My name is Chief Officer Shun Gon Pat. You're going to make me a rich man."

TWENTY-TWO

One Day Later

The humidity was overwhelming as Sierra stepped off the plane at Phuket International Airport. She wiped her brow. She'd always wanted to come to Thailand, but not for official business. Perhaps a honeymoon or a lover's vacation. Would that ever happen? she thought.

She met Sansor's police chief on the tarmac.

"You're from the CIA?" Chief Officer Shun Gon Pat asked.

Sierra showed her him her credentials. "You were in contact with my boss. Kate Price."

"Do you have the money?"

"Yes."

"We have the man you're looking for."

"Where is he?" she asked.

Gon Pat smiled. "Where's the ten thousand American dollars?"

"It will be wired to your account once we confirm our man is alive."

"He broke one my officer's wrists."

"Do you want the ten thousand or not? I'm not the one you should be bargaining with. I am just here to pick him up."

Gon Pat shrugged. "It was worth a try," he said. "Follow me."

She went with Gon Pat to the police station and followed him to his office. He held the door open for her, and she walked inside.

Then she saw him.

"Jason!" she said. "I can—"

Drake was sitting close to Gon Pat's desk. His wrists were cuffed. He didn't look up when he heard Sierra's voice.

"Surprise, surprise," Drake said.

Gon Pat sat down at his desk. He nodded at the officers who'd escorted him and Sierra into the room. "You can leave," he said in Thai.

They left.

Once they were gone, he stood up and removed the cuffs from Drake's wrists. He made his way back to his desk and sat down again. He looked at the two Americans that had made his otherwise peaceful city less peaceful.

"I want another ten thousand," Gon Pat said to Sierra. "I want it or I make this an international news story."

"That's ridiculous," she said. "I already told you, I'm not the one you should be bargaining with. I didn't arrange this."

"You're CIA. You're American. You have money and I know you can get it so don't play dumb."

Drake chuckled.

Sierra pulled out her phone and sent a message to Price. "I asked for more. No guarantees."

"Good," the police chief said. He clapped his hands, opened a drawer in his desk, and pulled out a cigar. He lit it up.

"Jason, I'm sorry they had to pull you in like this," Sierra said. "Did they hurt you?"

"They didn't pull me in," Drake said—his voice was low, guttural. It sounded like he was doing everything in his being to stop himself from doing something irrational. "I let them take me."

"What?" Sierra looked confused.

Gon Pat laughed. "We didn't have to find him. He came looking for us. He knew you were coming. He's a smart guy."

"Why didn't you run?" Sierra's said.

"A hunch," Drake said. His eyes glowed in the dark of the room. Shades of green, blue, and turquoise. "What do you want?"

"This was Kate's idea, bringing you in like this. When we found out you were in Thailand, she ... This is the only way she thought we could pull you in."

"It worked."

"I'm sorry."

"How's Ruby?"

"You should know that she didn't talk. She was going to kill me."

That fact made Drake smirk. "Then why are you still alive?"

"She held a gun up to my head! If it wasn't for Houston, I would have been dead."

"Good boy," Drake said.

"I'm surprised that dog is still alive."

"The dog won't quit."

"Listen, Jason. I don't know what to say. Less than forty-eight hours ago, I thought you were dead. I didn't want to come here. I didn't want to look for you. You've already sacrificed so much for your country."

"So why did you come looking for me?"

"Your brother—"She stopped herself. She knew she couldn't say anymore in front of the police chief.

Drake froze when he heard the words. His jaw clenched. He turned from Sierra and mouthed the name *Colin*.

Sierra turned to Gon Pat and said, "We need privacy."

Gon Pat shrugged. "Why should I? This man broke an officer's wrist."

"I'll ask my boss for another five on top of the twenty," she said.

Gon Pat exhaled a thick plume of cigar smoke from his mouth and smiled. "Good," he said. He stood up and left the room.

Sierra's mouth felt dry. She looked at Drake with large, empathetic eyes. She knew she had to explain everything to him—there was no point in holding anything back. He had a knack for cutting through the bullshit.

"Well?" Drake grunted. "You said it's about my brother."

"Jason, I—"

"Don't apologize," he said. "You'll just look weak. Tell me what this is about. What do you mean, 'my brother?'"

"About a week ago, a group of Ukrainian special forces captured a man. He was a smuggler delivering chemical weapons to Crimean, anti-Russian forces. During interrogation, the man said your name."

"What?"

"According to an intercepted transcript, the man says he is your brother."

"You're lying."

"I'm not."

Sierra saw something in Drake's eyes she had never seen before. Was it weakness?

"Where is he?" Drake asked.

"He's being held in a facility in Kyiv. It's called Temny."

"How do we get inside?"

"You want to get him out?"

"I want to find out the truth."

"The man who interviewed your brother is Dr. Maxim Rachman. He's a psychologist and professor at Taras Shevchenko National University. Kate is sending me on this mission to meet with him. I didn't feel right meeting Doctor Rachman alone. She figured you'd want to know."

"If you're lying to me, I'll end you," Drake said.

"Do you honestly think I don't know that? Do you think I would take this risk? I'm not lying to you, Jason. Come with me, and I will show you the intercept. I'll show you everything I have."

"My brother is dead."

"I know," Sierra said. "I looked up everything. According to US military documents, your brother died in Iraq in 2003. But ..." Her voice trailed off.

Drake closed his eyes and went silent. He mulled over everything. He knew she wasn't lying.

"If you agree to come with me, you need to know that we have to move without rousing suspicion," Sierra said. "No one can know this is a CIA operation, understand?"

Drake nodded.

He was going to go with her.

He was going with her. He was going to find out if the man in Ukraine was actually his brother.

PART 2 - THE BROTHER

TWENTY-THREE

It'd been two days since the interrogation in Temny with the smuggler, and Maxim felt sick. He hated what he had become. He was a government tool. A weapon that they could use against their targets.

Still, what was he supposed to do? He had a young family. He had to provide for them. If he refused Oksi's orders, his entire world would fall apart.

He sat at his desk in his home office and tried not to think about it.

He knew it was only a matter of time before Oksi called him back to Temny to continue the interrogation.

He looked over the notes he'd taken during the interrogation.

While the man said he was a smuggler, he was more than that. He'd been trained. Ex-military? Special forces? There was something in his eyes that gave that glimmer of his past away.

Maxim's wife knocked on the door to his office.

"What is it?" he said, not looking away from his computer.

The door to his office slid open. His wife poked her head inside. "It's late. When will you be done?"

"This is important work," Maxim said, frustrated. "I can't stop now."

"You've been cooped up in this room for days. You haven't even come out to see your daughter—"

"Josephina, please!" Maxim snapped. "This is my work!"

"I worry for you," she said.

"I'm fine."

She bit her lower lip but didn't leave. "Did you tell Roman not to come back here?"

Maxim understood right away that it wasn't his work that was bothering her. It was his brother—and his unanticipated appearance at their house days earlier.

"He wanted to thank me for the job I got him. That's all."

"I don't trust him. Every time he shows up, you end up in trouble.
"

"He's my brother," Maxim said. "I had to help him. He came to look for help. He said he's changed."

"He took advantage of you before."

"He's changed."

Josephina shook her head. "I don't want you to make the same mistakes again. Your brother is not a good man. You should not have helped him."

"I can't talk about this right now," Maxim said. "Now, please. My love, I need to focus on my work."

"Of course," Josephina said. She closed the door to the office and left.

Maxim listened to her footsteps as they walked down the hallway. He shook his head. He couldn't think about such things. He needed to focus on what he could control, and all he could control were the questions he was going to ask the smuggler when they met again, whenever that was.

He read over his notes.

He'd gotten the smuggler to talk of his past. He'd need to push him more if he was going to find out who had hired him to deliver the weapons to the rebels. He'd need to administer more drugs, ask more questions. It made him feel sick.

TWENTY-FOUR

Artem shuffled along with the line at the customs booth in Kyiv International Airport. The airport was stuffed like a congested nostril. Hordes of tired travelers moved in thick and slow lines through a maze of queues. The man just ahead of Artem looked like he weighed more than three hundred pounds and shuffled his feet along the dirty floor as if on his death march. The man's waist sagged over the sides of his tight pants. He had thick yellow pit stains.

Artem turned away from the man with disgust. He looked around the airport; queue after queue were the same. There was no escape. Everywhere he looked was jam-packed with disgusting filth.

"Sir?" a woman's voice called to him. It was the clerk. It was finally his turn.

The customs officer was young and attractive. She had blonde hair and a small face. "Papers, please," she said in Ukrainian as Artem approached.

He looked at her neck. His hand would fit perfectly around it, he thought. Her skin was so pale already—would anyone notice if she was dead?

"Sir, your papers," she said again.

"Of course," Artem responded, shaking his head, slightly flustered by the thought of killing her. He pulled out the passport he'd picked up from the Company at the train station and slid it under the small hole in the booth.

The young woman opened the passport. She looked at the photograph and then up at Artem. "You come from Moscow?"

"Yes," Artem said.

"Your job?"

"I'm a climatologist. I measure the levels of carbon dioxide in our atmosphere. It's a dire situation," he said.

"So, you want to save the world?" She playfully smiled at him.

Artem smiled back. Women liked him. They liked his aloofness, his strangeness. They didn't realize that he was a spider—once in his web, he'd hurt them. He took a deep breath and tried not to think about strangling her. "The world is in bad shape," he said with a wry smile on his face. "I only want to help."

She blushed. "And how long will you be staying in Ukraine, Mr. Alexander?"

Alexander Kruschev was Artem's alias.

"After I attend the conference on climate change at Taras Shevchenko National University in one week, I will leave."

"You can go through," she said.

He winked at her and made his way out of the airport terminal. Once on the street, he hailed a cab.

"Take me to the Queen's Hotel," Artem said after getting inside the first cab that pulled up. "I need some rest."

TWENTY-FIVE

Drake and Sierra didn't speak much after they left the police station in Sansor. There wasn't much to talk about. They took a cab from the small village to Phuket International Airport. Drake looked out the window of the cab as it rolled through the lush Thai jungle. Another chapter of his life had closed.

He just hoped that Pok would be okay. The kid was tough, but the world can shatter even the strong if they aren't smart. Still, he had faith the kid would pull through.

Sierra had booked a commercial flight for the two of them, a Boeing 777 operated by Thai Airlines. Their seats were first class. Drake hated first class—it was the smell. The colognes and perfumes bothered him.

Almost an hour after their meeting with the police chief, Sierra handed Drake the intercept while they both took their seats in the airplane.

He read through it, handed it back to her, and closed his eyes.

Colin.

Memories of his past stormed into his mind. Again.

Sierra knew to leave him alone.

Drake thought of the day he found out his brother was dead.

It was autumn and unusually cold in Texas. He was on his bed and was reading about photosynthesis, how plants transformed the sun's light into energy. He remembered thinking about that, turning something natural into something amazing. Something as essential and ordinary as sunlight was powerful enough to give life to an entire planet.

His mom knocked on his door. Her fists slammed against the door in an unusual manner.

He remembered it being especially odd because, when he opened the door and saw her, he didn't smell alcohol on her breath. There was a look on her face that didn't seem right.

"He's gone," she said, her lower lip trembling.

"Who's gone?" Drake asked.

"Colin."

Drake didn't know what she meant. He stood silent.

His mother held a letter. He snatched it from her hands and read its contents. He seethed, yet he remained in control. It was a strange feeling.

The letter was from the US military. Colin was dead.

Drake looked at his mother and felt both anger and sadness. How could she be so stupid? How could she not see that it was her actions that had led to this?

He didn't have time to come to any conclusion.

The front door to the house opened. Dave was home. "What the hell is going on?" he yelled.

Drake's mother walked downstairs. Drake followed her.

Dave's face was beet red. He'd been drinking. "Why are the lights out? What's going on?"

"Dave, it's about Colin—" Drake's mother said, dropping to her knees.

Dave saw her and Drake at the base of the stairwell. He saw the letter in Drake's hands.

Drake stared at Dave defiantly. He thought about everything; his pain, his sorrow, his confusion.

"What's that in your hand?" Dave said.

"It's your death sentence," Drake said. "You did this. You did this to all of us."

Dave burped. "You little pansy. I'm going to beat the shit out of you." He looked at Drake's mother. "But not before I put you in your place."

Drake's mother was lost in sorrow. She couldn't even put together a sentence. She'd just discovered her oldest son was dead. How could she think or act rationally?

Dave walked up to her. "You bitch."

"Colin is dead," Drake shouted. "You need to leave."

"Shut up!" Dave screamed. "I'm not talking to you. I'm talking to your skank-ass mother. I'm tired of both of you. I've been putting up with this shit for long enough."

"You need to leave," Drake said. "My mother is grieving."

His mother's cries reverberated through the house, grief-stricken echoes of pain and anguish. She could hardly breathe. It looked like she was in immense pain, like she was being tortured.

"Get up!" Dave said to her.

"My boy," she said, looking at Dave. Her words were full of snot and tears.

"If you don't leave now, I'll hurt you," Drake said.

Dave turned to Drake. "What did you say, boy?"

"You heard what I said."

Drake readied himself for an attack. He figured Dave was going to strike at him. Instead, Dave walked up to him and reached for the letter. He snatched it from Drake's hand and read it.

A smile crept along his face. "The little asshole is dead? Thank god. That kid was a blight. A damn curse."

"You watch what you say," Drake said.

"Or what?"

"Or I'll kill you."

Dave mockingly held the letter up in the air. "I should frame this. This is a vindication. Both you boys are nothing but trouble. You were shit kids. And while your pathetic mother is partially to blame, your father holds the brunt of the blame. He was weak—he was pathetic! How did he die again? A hit and run?"

Drake charged Dave. He'd lost all control. The future, the hope that one day he'd be out of the house, no longer mattered to him. He just wanted to hurt Dave.

Dave's wide frame easily bore the brunt of Drake's first levy of attacks. He simply brushed them aside and paid them little notice. He fought back. His thick fingers dug deep into Drake's left bicep and twisted his wrist so that Drake's arm bent out of shape. Drake had no choice but to move with the motion. If he didn't, his arm would have been dislodged from its socket. Drake fell to his knees and grimaced.

"Do you give up?" Dave screamed.

Drake, anguished and trying his best to push through the pain, didn't respond. Dave wasn't going to let go, though. "Do you give up, you little piece of shit? You foul little monster. I should have killed you boys long ago. It's a shame you couldn't have gone with your brother. All I wanted was your mother and the fat pension from your dead father."

Drake threw an uppercut toward Dave's jaw.

His drunk step-father let go and stumbled backward, shocked by the strength in the fifteen-year-old's arm. The force of the punch made him bite his tongue, and a pool of blood shot out from his mouth. "You mongrel!" Dave said.

Drake stared at Dave and kept still. He lifted his fists. In his peripheral vision, he saw his mother—cowering on the floor, crying, still overwhelmed by the news she'd received and probably not fully realizing what was happening.

Dave gathered his balance. "I'm going to kill you," he said. Threatened and drunk, he acted out in anger and rage. He pulled out a pistol hidden in his jacket and aimed it at Drake.

The sight of the gun seemed to snap Drake's mother out of her stupor. She stood up.

"I'll kill you," Dave said. "If you make one more move, I'll kill you."

"Don't!" Drake's mother screamed.

Drake stared at the gun. He felt calm. He didn't feel scared. He stared at the barrel of the gun and at Dave.

Dave's hand wobbled in the darkness of the house. "Get ready to die, boy!"

The moonlight that cut through the window danced along the walls and floor. Drake's mother's movements disappeared into odd shadows. Dave didn't see her coming. She put her hands on Dave's arms.

"You whore!" he shouted.

Drake seized the advantage. As his mother and Dave fought, he charged forward. He tackled his step-father to the ground.

Dave, falling, pulled down on the trigger.

The gun fell from Dave's hand as his back hit the floor. Drake, panicked, reached for it. It seemed instinctive. He held it up—aiming the pistol at Dave. Drake hadn't yet realized how bad the situation was.

"Stand down!" Drake shouted.

Police sirens echoed out on the street. The neighbors had clearly heard the ruckus.

"Are you okay, Mom?" Drake said.

There was no response.

He looked at his mother. She was on her stomach.

"Are you okay?"

He then saw it. A pool of blood leaked from beneath her body.

Dave was on his back, resting against the hallway wall.

Drake closed his eyes. The bastard had taken his brother and now his mother.

He pulled down on the trigger and put two bullets in Dave's stomach.

SIERRA PUSHED Drake's arm until he woke up.

His dreams had made him speak aloud. Others in first class had noticed.

"What's wrong?" she asked.

Drake shook his head. "I'm sorry," he said.

"We're about to land."

Drake rubbed his head. "Okay."

When their flight had landed, he and Sierra spoke again.

"I have arranged a meeting with Dr. Rachman at his office tonight," she said. "Are you going to be okay? I don't think I've ever seen you like this."

"Yes," Drake said. "I'll be fine."

The two of them left the airport, got into a cab, and made their way to the university.

TWENTY-SIX

A flurry of rain pattered against Artem's hotel window. It was five p.m. and already dark outside. Heavy storm clouds had formed over Kyiv since his arrival. According to weather reports, the bad weather was going to last for days.

Artem was going over operational details. The documents he'd picked up from the Company were spread out on his hotel bed. He examined each one of them carefully.

There was the photograph of the target, a detailed schematic of the Temny Facility where he was being held, and some information about vulnerable individuals who worked within the facility.

The Company had information on everybody and everything. It made Artem's job too easy—almost to the point that he found it boring.

Like a complex puzzle, he put the pieces together. The facility was in an old building, but one that had been heavily modified with advanced surveillance systems. There were over one thousand security cameras in the facility.

Getting into the building would be difficult enough, but getting to the target would be another problem altogether. He'd have to think outside the box.

He knew the only way he'd get to the target with any kind of confidence would be if he shut down all electronic equipment in the facility. To do that, he'd need someone on the inside to do his bidding.

He looked at the picture of a janitor—underneath, in black marker, were the words, 'Roman Rachman--newly hired.'

Artem rubbed his chin. He flipped the picture over and read the details about the janitor.

Roman was a gambler, and he frequented a bar called The Ruins. It was located in the middle of Kyiv. He owed a Russian gang one million Russian rubles. The gang had tried to kill Roman over a decade ago, but he was patient. He'd kept a low profile for over a decade.

Artem put the picture in his back pocket. Roman would be his way inside.

He walked to his computer and looked up the address of the bar.

He left the hotel and walked to The Ruins.

Before going inside, he looked at the image of the janitor once more.

It didn't take him long to find Roman. The newly hired Temny janitor was boisterous. He was at the bar, had three empty pint glasses in front of him, and was trying to make bets with everyone around him. A football match was on.

Artem sat down beside him. "Who's playing?" he asked.

"Manchester City and Arsenal," Roman said. His eyes were glazed, and his breath smelled of lager.

"Do you want to bet on who the winner is?" Artem asked.

Roman finished a pint and looked at the man. "How much?"

"How about the debt you still owe the Chevka gang?"

Roman froze. His skin turned pale. "Who ... who are you?"

"I know many things about you," Artem said. "I know you are a gambler, for one."

"Are you from the Chevka?"

Artem chuckled. "I am not from the Chevka, but I can make sure they never bother you again," he said.

"I have a job now," Roman said. "It's a good job. It pays well. I don't need your help."

"I don't think you understand," Artem said. "This isn't about helping you. You are going to do what I say, and I am going to clear up your debt with the Chevka."

"No!" Roman said. He stood up from the bar, but stopped when Artem grabbed his wrist. He winced in pain. Artem's grip was strong.

"Let go," Roman said. "It hurts."

"Come walk with me. We have much to discuss. If you don't, I'll kill everyone you love."

Roman hesitated. He wanted to say no, but he'd met men like Artem before. He knew when they were serious. He left the bar with Artem.

They walked through the streets of Kyiv. The rain had stopped, filling the streets with fog. Large puddles had formed along the street curbs.

"Where are we going?" Roman asked. "I have work in the morning. I need to get home. I need to sleep."

Artem didn't answer. He just kept walking.

They walked for thirty minutes, almost entirely in silence. By the time they got to their destination, it was clear to Roman what Artem wanted.

Artem had taken them to Temny.

"Who are you?" Roman asked.

"Do you work here?" Artem asked.

Roman nodded.

"I need you to get me inside."

"I'm a janitor," Roman said. "That's all I am. I can't get you inside. If you want to get inside, you should—" He stopped himself. "I can't get you inside."

"I don't care about your brother," Artem said.

"You know my brother works here?"

"Yes," Artem said. "The people who hired me know a lot of things. I know about your brother, and I know he has a family. If you help me, he'll be fine."

"How can I help you?"

"I have a plan to get inside, a plan that you will help me with."

"This is a government facility," Roman said. "You need clearance. It's going to be difficult to procure."

Artem rubbed his head. "Just listen. If you don't, I will kill your brother and his family."

Roman tried to swallow but couldn't. He felt beyond sick. Heavy rain began to fall again, soaking his clothes. The lights from the facility glowed ominously through the rain and made the stone walls of Temny glisten. He knew what he had to do. "Okay," he said. "I'll help you."

Artem went with Roman to his apartment that night. The two of them went over every detail. It was going to be a multi-pronged attack.

"You're going to help build a bomb inside the facility's electrical room. A bomb that will shut down every piece of electronic equipment inside."

"Build a bomb?"

"You'll be making what's called an EPFCG inside. You'll be taking it in, piece by piece. I'll instruct you how to build it. You'll have to make sure you hide it from the guards and officers in the building. Put it inside a janitor closet. It will be small."

"What does EPFCG mean?"

"It's a device that will shut down the facility's electrical system."

"What are you going to do?"

"Nothing that concerns you," Artem said. "And remember, if you run or go to the police, I will murder your brother and his family."

Roman nodded.

Artem left Roman's apartment and walked back to his hotel. All he had do to now was procure the materials to build the bomb. To do that, he'd have to call the Company.

TWENTY-SEVEN

Working at a university and at a military prison made Maxim feel like he was living two different lives. One was academic and liberal, one conservative and cold. It left him feeling like a man often at odds with himself. He didn't know which life he identified with more. Was he the man who'd promised his life to help those in need with their mental suffering? Or was he just a robot who did what he was told to get what he wanted?

While he wanted to push himself away from it all, he couldn't give up the money from Commander Oksi. He had to do what he had to do. He had to support Josephina and his child. They were all that mattered. They mattered more than his soul. Didn't they?

It was close to eight p.m., and he was inside his university office. He sat at his desk, reading over his students papers. Their last assignment concerned an analysis of Sigmund Freud's papers on hysteria and fear. They were to compare them against Carl Jung's work on the same subject.

A student quoted Jung's work, *Symbols of Transformation*.

'The neurotic who tries to wiggle out of the necessity of living wins nothing and only burdens himself with a constant foretaste of aging and dying, which must appear especially cruel on account of the total emptiness and meaningless of his life.'

He put down the paper and rubbed his brow. Was he the neurotic? he wondered. Had he forgot what life was about? Living?

His phone rang.

"Hello?"

"It's Commander Oksi."

"What do you want?"

"Two days."

"Two days?"

"I want you to come back to Temny in two days for the second ..." Oksi paused. "*Interview.*"

"But—"

It didn't matter what Maxim said. It was too late. Oksi had hung up.

Maxim stared at his phone. He wanted to scream.

When it rang again he almost jumped out of his seat.

"What do you want from me?" he said, his voice strained and panicked.

"Two people are here to see you," his secretary said. "Is everything okay? You seem upset."

Maxim shook his head and cleared his throat. "I'm fine. Just busy. Who are they?"

"They are the ones that I told you about, sir. The ones from Harvard University."

"Can they come tomorrow?" he asked. "I'm actually not in the mood."

"They say it's urgent. They've come a long way."

Maxim looked at the picture of his family on his desk. Perhaps these people from Harvard could provide him with a way out, he thought. Perhaps they were his escape from Oksi's grip. "Send them in," he said.

"Of course."

Seconds later, he was greeted by the two individuals from

Harvard. One was tall. One was beautiful. Neither of them looked friendly, and he knew right away he'd made a mistake.

"Apologies for our late arrival," the beautiful one said. She sat down, and crossed her legs seductively, and glared at him. "This is very important."

The tall one remained silent and sat beside her. He had a mean look on his face and stared at Maxim with an intimidating coldness.

"What's this about?" Maxim asked, trying to play coy but failing.

"My name is Veronica Rose," Sierra said. "I'm from Harvard University." She pulled a card from her purse and handed it to Maxim.

He looked at the card. It looked official. He quickly typed her name into his computer's web search. Her face and profile came up—everything checked out.

"I don't want to be rude, but I am tired. Will this be quick?" Maxim said. "It's late and I just want to go home."

Sierra smiled. "Of course," she said. "This will be quick. We're here to offer you a job. One at Harvard. You just have to help us."

"Could this not be discussed over the phone or email? I'm a very busy man."

"No," Drake grunted.

"And who are you?" Maxim said. "You don't look like the typical Harvard recruiter, if you don't mind me saying."

Drake didn't react. He maintained his placid stare at Maxim. "Your office is disorganized, cluttered," he said. "For someone who analyzes the mind, you hardly seem to have your own house in order."

Maxim smiled awkwardly. There was something about Drake that unnerved Maxim. He'd looked into the eyes of many killers during his analysis of soldiers with PTSD. The tall man sat across from him was a killer, of that he was certain. He turned to Sierra. "Ms. Rose, if this is how Harvard does its business—offering a job through ridicule and embarrassment—then I want nothing to do with it. I need to go home to my wife."

Sierra shot Drake a disapproving look and then turned back to Maxim with an apologetic expression. "Perhaps we should leave your office," she said. "I'm sensing that a change of scenery might make us all feel more comfortable. You could call your wife and tell her you'll be late. You'll want to hear our offer."

Maxim closed his eyes. There was strain in her voice. She was hiding something from him. She was lying. "What is this about?"

"What do you mean?" Sierra asked, confused.

"I mean, I've been applying to universities in the United States for years. What is this about? Why now? Why does Harvard want anything to do with me now?"

Drake spoke up. "I recommend that you come with us, Professor. We'll buy the drinks."

Maxim knew then and there that it wasn't about Harvard. He'd been had. Still, he played along. "I know a place," he said. "It's called The Perogi Bar. It's near campus."

"Good," Sierra said.

TWENTY-EIGHT

The students at the university jokingly referred to The Perogi Bar as the *Soft Perogi*—they went for the drinks, not the food.

A group of students stood outside its entrance as Drake, Sierra, and Maxim approached.

Drake and Sierra stood three yards back from Maxim, far enough that they knew their whispers couldn't be heard. It helped that it was raining. The lashing rain and howling wind made it difficult to hear anything even a few inches from your face.

"If he doesn't give us access, we need to come up with a plan B," Drake whispered to Sierra. "Do you have one?"

Drake was so close to Sierra, she could smell his aftershave. "We will get access," she whispered back. "He has to help us. Remember, we need to do this without attracting any attention to the CIA. He's our best angle."

Drake grunted in frustration. He didn't mind playing along, but everything was beginning to feel a little too inconvenient. There were too many hurdles to overcome, too many obstacles in the way. Too many things that needed to go right. Still, he had to let Sierra move about and play the role of spy for now. When push came to shove and the hard decisions needed to be made, he'd do what he had to do.

Maxim stopped at the bar's entrance. "No one will pay attention to us in here," he said, holding the front door to the bar open for Sierra.

"Is it quiet?" Sierra asked him, walking inside.

"It's a student bar," Maxim said. "But if you want to discuss what I think you want to discuss, then this will be the best place. It will be quiet to ears who want to listen."

"Sounds like you're finally putting things together," Drake said. "Maybe you're not as dumb as I thought."

Maxim shook his head. "You don't know anything about me," he said. "You're an arrogant American. You've been sent here to bully me. For what reason, I'd like to know."

Sierra thought about punching Drake in the arm but stopped herself. "My associate is awfully rude," she said to Maxim. "He sometimes doesn't know when to shut up."

Maxim shrugged. "You can stop the act," he said. He had a defeated look on his face. "Just talk to me straight—what do you want? And I expect you to pay for the drinks."

Drake turned to Sierra and nodded. His expression was plain. "We need to tell him who we are. He's already sniffed us out."

"Okay," Sierra said. "Once we sit down, we'll tell him everything."

A waitress met them at the entrance and guided them to a quiet and dark corner of the bar, one far enough away from the pounding speakers that they'd be able to at least hear each other talk. Russian rap music blasted through the bar.

Drake sat down and looked around. The walls of The Perogi were adorned with pictures of the Soviet rule of Ukraine during World War II. There were posters of Soviet Union propaganda. Soviet Ukraine was one of the constituent republics of the Soviet Union from the Union's inception in 1922 until its break-up in 1991. Of the 24 million combatants and civilians the Soviet Union lost during World War II, almost seven million of them were Ukrainians. Despite the losses, despite the pain the country and its people endured, Ukraine was one of the last Soviet territories to declare its independence from Communist Russia. It took a nuclear meltdown in Chernobyl and the continued Russification of policies for the people to realize that they needed new leadership and change. Many of the photographs on the walls depicted Ukrainian soldiers—their forlorn and hopeless faces hit Drake hard. They were fighting against true evil, the Nazis, but they were fighting on behalf of another evil, the Soviet Union—evil against evil. Bad men fighting bad men with good men. The thought irritated Drake like a stone in his boot.

He turned to Maxim once they were all sat down and comfortable. There was no point in beating around the bush. He wanted to find out if Maxim was one of the good men or not. "You're an interrogator at Temny?"

Maxim froze." What? What do you mean?"

"The prisoner you've interrogated," Drake said. "He said my name."

"What?"

"Stop playing dumb," Drake said. "You—"

Sierra cut him off. She glared at Drake with a certain kind of contempt that made Drake like her more. She was a fighter, and she was doing her damn best to keep the operation together. "We're not from Harvard," she said to Maxim.

"No shit," Maxim said. "Where are you from? How do you know about ... ?" His voice trailed off. He didn't want to admit it himself.

"We're intelligence officers from a foreign agency," she said.

"She's CIA," Drake said, cutting her off. "She knows everything about you."

Sierra kicked Drake under the table and snarled at him. It almost turned him on, how combative she was. She really wanted things to go her way.

"I'm... We're not... You need to understand." She was flustered. She didn't know what to do or say. Drake was foiling her entire plan.

The waitress appeared at their table. "What can I get you?" she asked in Ukrainian.

"Three pilsners," Drake responded in her native tongue.

The waitress left. Maxim stared at Drake with awe and horror. "Who are you?" he asked. "You speak Ukrainian?"

"I'm not CIA," Drake grunted. "That's all you need to know."

"Why are you here?" Maxim asked.

"Because she said you're interrogating my brother."

"You're Jason Drake?"

Drake nodded.

Maxim was coming to terms with it all. His expression transformed from one of shock to one of dismay.

"We need to speak to the prisoner," Sierra said. "Privately, if possible. You need to get us into Temny. If you get us a private meeting with the prisoner, we'll get you the job in Harvard."

Maxim looked around the cluttered, busy bar. It'd been built within an old townhouse that had been renovated numerous times. Each of the repurposed rooms within it were stuffed with drunk, clamoring students. He looked at Sierra and took a long swig of his pilsner, which the waitress had just placed in front of him. "I want assurances."

"You'll get them," she said. "We can make your dreams come true if you help us."

"I want my family out of this country. If Russia invades—if this whole region erupts into war—then this will be an awful place. I want out."

"We will get your family out if we have to."

Maxim looked at Drake. "He's your brother?"

Drake nodded.

"You do know he's a smuggler?" Maxim said. "He was delivering weapons to Ukrainian rebels who were going to use them against Russian soldiers."

"I know the details," Drake said.

"He said your name during the interrogation."

"Up until twenty hours ago, I thought my brother was dead," Drake said. "And in a way..." He took a sip of his beer. "In a way, I hope he is dead. I hope whoever you have in that prison or facility or whatever you call it isn't my brother. I hope the man you have in there is a liar."

"He is your brother," Maxim said.

Drake's eyebrow rose. "How can you be sure?"

"You have his eyes."

"So, you'll help us?" Sierra said.

"Yes," Maxim said, finishing his beer, then wiping his face. "I'll get you inside Temny. But it's a highly guarded facility—they'll ask many questions. I assume you can—"

"We can," Drake said. "We can do whatever you think we need to do. Just get us in there."

"Of course," Maxim said. "I'll do whatever you tell me to do if you get me that position at Harvard."

Sierra smiled. Despite everything that had gone wrong, she had still got what she wanted. She was going to find out what Drake's brother had to do with Ukrainian rebels and why he was giving them chemical weapons. "When do you meet with him next?" she asked Maxim.

"Two days," Maxim said, signaling to the waitress for another drink. "In two days, I am scheduled to interrogate him again. Meet me at the university. I'll make sure you both have clearance to join me."

TWENTY-NINE

After meeting with Maxim, Drake and Sierra headed to their hotel, which was located in the middle of Kyiv. It was called The Iris. It was a boutique hotel. Its rooms were large and mostly empty. Modern furniture and art decorated each room.

Drake didn't like it. When he got to the room Sierra had booked for them, he poured himself a glass of vodka and walked to the window. He looked down on the rainy streets of Kyiv with a depressed expression on his face.

Colin. His brother. Alive.

The streets of Kyiv were mostly empty. His attention focused on the buildings that surrounded the hotel.

The diverse and unique architecture of the capital of Ukraine featured a blend between the old and new: Soviet Modernism, Ukraine Baroque, and Art Nouveau. As one of the oldest cities in Europe, it featured beautiful cathedrals and palaces built well before the 18th century. And as one of the Soviet era's most cherished state entities, it featured dominating and oppressive Soviet architecture—prisons, government offices, and housing apartments dotted the city and gave its skyline a unique outline.

The Iris Hotel was located in the Shevchenkivs'kyi District of the city. A district close to Taras Shevchenko National University.

The one-bed room that Drake and Sierra were in was located on the fourth floor.

Sierra sat on the bed and watched the television. The BBC World News was on. The anchor spoke with a patronizing and elite British accent.

"Russian military forces continue to move to the border of Ukraine in a build-up of military strength not seen in Europe since World War II. While the European Union have criticized Russia's aggression, the United States has remained unusually quiet. The former adversary of the Soviet Union seems comfortable letting things happen as they will. American President, Roy Clarkson, said recently in an address relating to the hostilities in Europe that the United States will help foster a relationship of peace between the two nations. That the only option is peace."

Drake listened to the broadcast and grunted, "Turn it off."

"Why?" Sierra asked.

"Because it'll rot your brain."

"I'm just trying to stay informed. I haven't talked to Kate since I left the capital. I want to know what's going on."

"And you think the news will help you with that?"

"Yes, I do."

Drake shook his head. "I need another glass of vodka."

"I've never seen you drink this much."

"One day ago, I thought my brother was dead," he muttered under his breath, though loud enough for Sierra to hear. He walked to the liquor cabinet and poured himself another drink. "Then you showed up, telling me my brother was alive and that he was working as a smuggler for some Ukrainian rebels. That he's being held in some facility in Ukraine. I wanted to think you were lying. I was hoping this was a trap set by Kate to pull me back into the CIA."

"And now you realize that I was telling you the truth."

Drake shot back the glass he'd just poured. He placed the glass down and shook his head. He was done drinking for the night. "What is Kate up to?" he asked.

"She's been fired."

"What?"

"She was trying to convince President Clarkson to act on the Russian aggression in Ukraine. He disagreed with her."

"So, he fired her?"

"You know Kate."

Drake nodded. "I knew she wouldn't last long as Director."

"She seemed scared. Uncertain. She said she couldn't trust anyone. Why the hell do you think she sent me here?"

"Something is rotten in the capital," Drake said.

"I know! It's almost as Clarkson wants the Russians to invade Ukraine. The Russian President will see our hesitance as weakness."

Drake walked back to the window. A drunk man was stumbling down an alley. He was holding a bottle of vodka and using the old stone walls of buildings for balance. He fell to the ground. The bottle smashed into pieces. The man lay unconscious on the cement. A group of teenagers had seen him. They approached, but not to help. They took his wallet from his back pocket and ran off.

Drake shrugged. "Maybe President Roy Clarkson doesn't want to meddle in the affairs of foreign governments," he said. "Maybe he's chosen to be an isolationist. He did take a bullet in the neck at the beginning of his second term. Maybe he does want peace."

"You can't believe that."

"I don't know what I believe anymore."

"There's more to this. You know there is. Your brother, an American, was giving weapons to anti-Russian rebels. Something big is going down. And our government doesn't want to act—and, making matters worse, is punishing those who try to act!"

"There's always more than meets the eye," Drake said. "I agree with you on that. The President's response to Russian aggression doesn't add up. Why would he not want Kate to send a team in to investigate?"

"I don't know."

"I think we're fighting ourselves as much as we are fighting our enemies," Drake said. "There are enemies within and without. From my experience, it's always been follow-the-money. You need to ask yourself who benefits from a Russian invasion—that's the real threat here, isn't it? If the Russian rebels secured those weapons from my brother, they would have used them to bomb Russian troops. If they bombed Russian troops, then the Russian military's build-up at the border of Ukraine would be vindicated. Hell, even an invasion might be vindicated."

"That sounds like conspiracy," Sierra said. "Why doesn't President Clarkson intervene? You can't think that Clarkson and Makarov are working together."

"No," Drake said. "I don't think that. But I do want to know what's going on, and I think my brother can help."

Sierra turned off the news. "This whole world is so confusing," she said. "I knew I wasn't ready for this. I didn't want to come here. I was happy back at Langley, working the typical nine-to-five. I was satisfied, mostly. After what happened to my mother, I battled with panic attacks. I'm not fit for the field."

"You're doing fine," Drake said. "These assignments never go to plan."

Sierra looked at Drake. He was still looking out the window. "Thank you for coming," she said. "You could have easily run."

"I need to sleep," Drake responded. He walked toward the bathroom.

Sierra stood up from the bed and embraced him. "You're the only thing that seems solid in this whole world. Whenever I need reminding that there are still good people out there, I think of you."

"Stop being so dramatic," he said. "You know what I am."

"Stop pretending you're not a good person," she said.

He pulled her head close to his chest. "You clearly don't know anything about me," he said. "I'm a killer."

She looked up into his eyes. They were blue and bright. "There's goodness in you. I know there is. From the first day I met you, all those years ago, you have always reminded me that what we do at the CIA has a purpose. Even if you don't believe it."

She went to kiss him. He pulled away.

"Is it Ruby?" she asked.

"That woman has done a lot for me."

Sierra nodded. "I hope to find someone like you some day."

"Don't be foolish."

Sierra fell asleep on the bed.

Drake looked out the window of the hotel room. He couldn't sleep. His mind kept taking him back into his past. A past that he was about to face.

THIRTY

Maxim walked nervously through the packed streets of Kyiv. It had been less than an hour since he left The Perogi. He felt an impending sense of doom—like the world was about to come to an end. He'd just promised two individuals from a foreign intelligence agency that he would help them break into a government facility. He was about to commit treason. He didn't know how, but he was going to do it. He had to. It was his only way out.

Soaking wet from the rain, he decided he'd walked far enough. He hailed a cab and took it home.

After paying the cabbie, he walked into his house. Josephina was in the kitchen, waiting for him. It was almost midnight.

"You said you'd be home by dinner."

He looked at her, an expression of regret on his face. "I'm sorry," he said. "I forgot to tell you. I was met by two ..." Should he tell her the truth? No, he thought. He couldn't have her worried. "Recruiters," he said. "They came from Harvard." He tried to hide his panic. "They wanted to talk about a job prospect in the United States."

Josephina looked at him. She knew he was lying. "Ever since your brother came back into your life, you've been acting so strange."

"It's not about him," he said. "I promise it's not."

She approached her husband and smelled his breath. "You've been drinking."

"The recruiters wanted to talk at a bar."

"You don't like to drink."

"It was a celebration."

"And yet you don't seem happy."

He stepped away from Josephina and ran his hands through his longish hair. "This has nothing to do with my brother!" he said loudly. "You need to trust me." He said it too loudly. Upstairs, their young daughter began to cry.

"Great," his wife said. A scolding look appeared on her face. "Another night when I am the one left with taking care of our little one."

Josephina marched upstairs to attend their child.

Maxim poured himself a glass of water. As the glass filled, he closed his eyes. He was growing tired of living his double life. It wasn't for him. After finishing the glass, he took a few deep breaths and closed his eyes.

He'd help the CIA operatives.

He'd help his family.

He knew what he had to do.

The only way he could get what he wanted was to help them. If he wanted out of Oksi's control, he'd have to betray his country.

THIRTY-ONE

Drake and Sierra spent the next forty-eight hours in the hotel. They hardly talked. Both of their minds were focused on the mission, although for very different reasons.

They didn't leave the hotel room because they knew it was risky. If someone spotted them, if they got into trouble, it would undermine everything. The fact that they'd managed to make a deal with Dr. Rachman was already miracle enough in Sierra's eyes. Her first field operation was going better than expected.

Drake didn't mind laying low. In fact, he kind of preferred it. He agreed with Sierra that they needed to be careful. The less attention, the better.

Sierra watched the news to pass the time.

Drake spent most of his time looking out of the hotel window. He thought about what he was going to say to his brother. He wanted answers. How had he survived? Why was he smuggling weapons for Ukrainian rebels? Why didn't he reach out?

As rain pattered against the window, his thoughts wandered back to Sierra and the mission.

"Have you contacted Kate?" he asked

"No," Sierra said, hardly looking away from the television. She was in her underwear and laid on the bed. "Since her meeting with the President, she knows she's under constant observation. She also knows that she never had the support of most of the members of the CIA—that there are many people who are watching her, perhaps even listening in on her phone calls. She knows she has to be careful. This whole operation has to be done in silence."

"She's finally figuring it out she's not likable?" Drake said, a half-smile on his face.

"She's not a politician."

"No," he said. "She was never fit to be Director."

"She wasn't."

Drake walked up to Sierra and stood above her. Sierra glared up at him. "What are you doing, Jason?" She gave him a seductive grin.

He grabbed the remote from beside her and turned off the television.

"I was watching that," she said.

"I'm done with the news."

"Why?"

"You know why."

"Why don't you sleep with me?"

"I told you."

"She's too innocent for you."

"She almost killed you."

"But she didn't."

Drake growled in frustration. He was angry. Not at Sierra, but at everything.

He sat back down and counted down the hours until the operation.

—

On the day of the operation to infiltrate Temny, Drake woke up early. He showered, got dressed, and stared at Sierra, who was sleeping The sun hadn't risen, and the room was still dark.

He decided to go for a walk. He needed to clear his head. Since it was the day of the mission, he didn't care about compromising anything.

After asking the man at the door of the hotel where an open coffee shop could be found, he made his way out onto the streets. It was still raining, and the city seemed slathered in a dark fog.

He followed the doorman's directions: two lefts and a right. He found the coffee shop.

Inside, he ordered himself an Americano and checked the time. It was 7:30. The fog had lifted, and the sky turned a light pink.

He picked up a newly delivered paper and skimmed through the headlines.

'Russian Aggression
NATO Waits For American Response.'

It was clear. NATO wasn't going to do a damn thing until the US Army showed up. Drake theorized as to why President Clarkson would be acting with such strange reluctance. When the two of them had met years ago, Clarkson seemed like a man who wanted to change the world. Clearly, the attack on the capital and the years he'd spent in office had spoiled him. The ghouls in the capital had seemingly sucked the life out of the man that was once heralded as a change from the status quo. Instead, all America was left with was another president who acted in the interests of the corporations who were seemingly in control of everything.

After reading the paper and finishing his coffee, Drake left the shop and made his way back to the hotel.

Sierra was waiting for him in the lobby.

"You weren't supposed to leave the room without me?"

"I was bored."

"Well, I just got an update from Dr. Rachman."

"What is it?"

"He's secured our passes to the facility. Are you ready to walk to the University? Do you have everything you need?"

"Yes," Drake said.

"Then let's go. I've already checked out and made sure our room is empty. Here's your bag." She handed Drake the luggage he'd taken from Thailand.

The two of them left the hotel and made their way to the University.

THIRTY-TWO

Two days after meeting them in his university office, Maxim picked up Sierra and Drake at a bus stop close to his university's campus. He rolled slowly to a stop as he approached them and kept his head low.

Drake walked up to Maxim's car and opened the back door for Sierra. She got inside. He followed.

"The military believes you are my assistants. They verified your credentials from the ID you provided," Maxim said to Drake and Sierra as they settled. "But you'd better have your shit in order. If anything is wrong, they will arrest all of us."

"You need to calm down," Drake said. "They're going to be more suspicious of you than of us. You look like shit. Have you slept?"

"Sleep? How could I sleep? You asked me to sneak you into a government facility."

"And in return, you'll get a position at Harvard," Drake grunted.

Maxim drank some coffee from a thermos in his cup holder and shook his head. He spilled some of the coffee on his car's leather seats. "Goddamnit," he said, frustrated. "This is all a mess."

"Take a deep breath," Sierra said. "Jason is right. I'm more worried about you than us. Our credentials are foolproof—you needn't worry. The papers will work. Remember, I'm CIA. I can help you."

"I've worked for Temny for years," Maxim said. "But they don't know my face. Every time I pull up to that facility, it's a new man at the entrance. You need to understand that I always get questioned. And if we get a young soldier at the gate, a young man who asks too many questions, well, then that could screw us over. Couldn't it?"

"It won't," Sierra said.

"It may even work to our advantage," Drake said.

"How?" Maxim asked.

"Just do what we tell you to do," Drake said. "I have a way of convincing people to do what I tell them to do."

Maxim looked at Drake in the rearview mirror and sighed. He was risking it all. For money? For his family? He didn't know.

He drove them from the university to Temny. He needed to find out who he was.

About thirty minutes after leaving the campus grounds, they arrived at their location. Temny was in the heart of the city.

Maxim rolled down his window as the officer operating the gate approached. The young officer was weaponless. As per usual, Maxim had never seen him before.

He was new.

The officer leaned down to the driver's seat window and looked at Maxim and then at the two passengers in the backseat. He had a suspicious expression on his face, his eyebrows furrowed, and he wasn't smiling. He spoke to Maxim in Ukrainian. "Who are they?" the officer said. The question seemed to be as much an accusation as anything else.

"Associates," Maxim said to the officer. "They're colleagues from America. Check with your superiors. They should have all the information you need. I sent it yesterday."

"I want to see their IDs."

"Of course."

Sierra handed Maxim her and Drake's identification papers.

Maxim handed the officer the papers. The officer took them and walked back to his booth.

Inside the car, Maxim began to sweat.

"You need to calm down," Sierra said. "Everything will be fine. The ID will check out."

"I have a daughter. I have a wife. They rely on me for everything —everything. Do you know how suspicious this is? How insane and dumb this is? I could lose everything if this goes wrong. I can't believe what I'm doing right now," Maxim said.

"You did perfectly," Sierra said, trying to reassure Maxim. "It's going to be okay. The papers I gave you will work."

The officer returned to the car. He leered at Drake and Sierra and then finally back at Maxim. He handed the papers back. "You're good to go," he said. "Stay well, Professor."

Maxim nodded at the officer and then placed both his hands on the steering wheel. He felt his heart pound in his chest. For a brief moment, he worried that he was experiencing a heart attack—his chest felt tight, and the pains were sharp. He took a deep breath and pushed through the pain.

The thick metal gate opened and gave him entrance to Temny. When the light signaled that it was safe to enter, Maxim drove inside.

While he drove down the narrow roads of the facility to the main building's parking garage entrance, Drake studied the buildings and routes he'd need to take if shit hit the fan.

He figured it would.

Maxim guided his car down the slope of the underground parking garage. He slid his keycard through a reader at the doors and waited for them to open.

"I don't know what happens next," Maxim said. "The commander in control of this facility gave you authorization. He didn't tell me anything else. This could be a trap. If they suspect—"

"They won't suspect a thing," Drake said. "Trust the process. You got us in. All you have to do now is take us to my brother. After that— after our discussion—we will leave. In one week, you and your family will be on US soil."

"You'd better not be lying to me," Maxim said.

"I'm not," Drake said.

Sierra looked at Drake nervously. She noticed his pupils. They seemed narrow and focused. He was in a headspace that she'd never seen before. She knew he was lying to Maxim. She knew that deep down, Drake felt everything was happening too easily.

THIRTY-THREE

Roman got dressed and looked at himself in the mirror. He felt sick. The man, *the assassin*, who'd confronted him days earlier had just sent him a text message.

Today is the day. You know what to do. The bomb is ready?

Roman responded to the text: *yes*. He then made himself a coffee and made his way down the stairwell to his truck. He placed his coffee in the cup holder and drove to Temny.

Fifteen minutes later, he checked in through the front gates and parked his truck in the underground garage.

He grabbed a duffel bag from his truck and made his way up to the maintenance shed. It was a small building about twenty yards from the main gate. Inside were his mop and cleaning supplies.

He tossed the duffel bag on the floor and then wheeled out his mop bucket. He dragged the bucket to the main building.

The hallways were jam-packed with military officials and facility personnel. Roman pushed his bucket down the dimly lit halls and stopped in front of the service elevators. His head pounded, and he felt sick. He was helping a foreign actor gain access to a military facility. He was betraying his brother's trust. Again.

As he waited for the elevator, a young officer bumped into him, causing him to spill his coffee.

"Get out of the way," the officer said.

Roman wanted to respond, but he held his tongue. He nodded at the officer apologetically and used his mop to clean up the spilled coffee from the tiled floor. When he was done cleaning it up, the elevator dinged, and the door opened. He waited for those inside to leave, and then rolled his mop into the elevator.

He was alone in the elevator.

He pushed the button for the door to close and then hit the button for his destination: electrical.

The bomb he'd constructed was inside the electrical closet.

As the elevator descended, he reminded himself why he was helping the assassin. He was doing it to protect his brother ... he was doing it to clear his name. This wasn't a matter of betrayal—this was a matter of survival.

The elevator doors opened. Roman rolled his mop out and made his way toward the electrical room. It was time to ignite the bomb.

Once inside the electrical room, he looked at what was left of the EPFCG device he'd built. It was an odd-looking construction—amateur. Wires and metal tubes splayed out in all directions. But that was the way it had to be. Roman wasn't an expert. The direction that the assassin had given him had understood his deficiencies. The assassin just needed the bomb to work. Roman did his best. He didn't know anything about electronics.

He dragged the bomb out of the closet. He flipped a switch. The EPFCG smoked and sparked.

Nervously, Roman looked around the electrical closet.

As Artem had promised, the bomb did not explode. Instead, it had fired off an electromagnetic pulse that shut down all electronics in the building and probably across the street.

The lights in the electrical closet turned off. The room and the hallway went dark.

The bomb he'd built had fried all the circuit boards and power in the building. It would have almost been like the facility was struck by a thousand bursts of lightning all at the same time.

Thanks to the EMP blast, all computers and security cameras would be shut down permanently. They'd have to be replaced.

Roman grabbed his mop and bucket, and walked them out of the room. He had to move quickly. He had to meet Artem up in the upper levels—near the holding cells. After that, it would all be done.

He walked to the stairwell and began the trek up to the fourth floor.

THIRTY-FOUR

Artem knew that Roman would do what he was told. The asshole was weak. He'd met men like him numerous times in his life. Men who'd been too scared to stand up for themselves, who would bend when questioned, when asked to act. They'd murder their own mother if pressed. Roman was one of those men.

The profile on the janitor at Temny from the Company was all Artem needed to confirm that Roman was the only way inside the heavily fortified facility.

Roman was a coward. Weak. Vulnerable. His history as a gambler and connections to mobsters and gangs in Russia and Ukraine was all the leverage Artem needed to use against him.

He was the perfect target.

The fact that his brother worked at Temny and had pulled some strings to get him a job only made Artem's job easier.

Artem stood on the street across from the facility. He was dressed in a long coat, wore a backpack, and smoked a cigarette. He'd been watching Roman from the shadows all morning. Tracking him after he'd left his apartment. If Roman failed to do his part, he knew he'd have to cancel the operation and reassess.

But deep down, he knew that Roman wouldn't fail.

After Roman entered the facility, Artem waited fifteen minutes.

He then tossed his half-smoked cigarette onto the ground and walked toward the entrance gate.

The guard who'd let Roman inside was sitting back at his booth. He had a sports magazine in his hand and casually flipped through the pages.

Artem stood outside the booth and looked at his digital watch. It wasn't to count the seconds. It was to see if it stopped working.

When his watch screen froze, he knew the bomb had gone off. He knew it was time to act.

THIRTY-FIVE

Artem's watch was dead. The lights on the street outside Temny flickered and went dark. People walking down the street looked at their phones with confusion. The screens were nothing more than black mirrors now. The EMP device had shut everything down.

The guard in the booth looked confused. All the monitors in his small four-by-four booth had gone dark. He picked up his mic to call into the facility, but he heard nothing in response, not even static. Confused, he walked out of the booth.

"Something wrong?" Artem asked the guard.

The two men were alone on their side of the street.

"The power. It's out," the guard said.

"Is it?"

Artem walked up to the guard, who was looking up and down the street, checking to see if other buildings had been affected by the power outage. He put his arm around the guard and said, "I'm holding a pistol to your back. Do what I say or die?"

"Okay, okay!" the guard said, his voice strained.

"Walk to the booth."

The guard did what Artem asked him to do. "There are security cameras everywhere in here. It's only a matter of time before they see you," the guard said. "You should leave."

"Get in the booth," Artem said.

The guard and Artem walked inside.

"Didn't you hear me? This is a government facility. There are armed guards inside. The cameras have already spotted you. You're wasting your time!"

Artem kicked the guard—the kid was getting on his nerves. The guard fell to his knees.

"The security cameras have been de-activated," Artem said. He looked at the computer monitors in the guard's booth. "Are you blind? The power is out!"

"There's a backup generator," the guard said. "Please don't kill me. If you leave, I will say that nothing happened. I promise."

Artem chuckled. "Your backup generator is gone, too. Everything is gone."

"How? What's going on? Were you responsible for that power outage?"

"Yes," Artem said. "And I no longer need you."

He shot the guard in the chest, killing him instantly.

He slid the body under a desk in the booth and searched it for any access keys—since the electronics in the facility were all down, he'd have to rely on older, more traditional means of entry.

Artem left the booth and walked up to the facility's gates. He scaled them without anyone on the street noticing—they were all still looking at their phones.

Artem dropped to the concrete ground inside the facility.

The guards inside were no better than the civilians on the other side of the wall. They looked confused—their earpieces weren't working, neither were their phones. The whole facility seemed to be in a state of hysteria. They didn't notice the intruder.

Artem smirked. The world had become too reliant on technology.

He almost casually walked toward the outdoor maintenance shed —the one where Roman had left the duffel bag. Using the key taken from the guard, Artem opened the door to the shed.

He went inside and closed the door behind him. He knelt down and opened the bag Roman had left. Inside was another explosive device.

Artem set a timer on the bomb for fifteen minutes. He then took off the backpack he was wearing and pulled out a pair of janitor's overalls. He put them on and clipped on Roman's name tag. He stuck the pistol he was carrying under his overalls and left the shed, pulling along a mop and bucket.

He made his way toward the main building.

As he left the shed, facility personnel ran past him, ignoring him. No one knew yet what exactly had gone on. Artem figured it would take them ten to fifteen minutes, but that was why he had the bomb in the shed. It would create further confusion and give him enough time to get out.

He used the security guard's keys to open a back door to the main building and stepped inside.

Red emergency lights flashed. Facility personnel ran up and down the halls. He listened to their conversations.

"What's going on?" one of them said.

"Where's the power?" said another.

Artem made his way to the stairwell. He walked to the holding cells. He had less than fifteen minutes to kill the smuggler and get out.

THIRTY-SIX

The walk up to the holding cells was interrupted when the red emergency lights turned on. The hallways had gone completely dark save for the intermittent, red, strobe-like flashing.

Maxim, who was guiding Drake and Sierra to the holding cells, froze. Drake walked into the scared psychologist.

"Keep moving," Drake said, frustrated. "Aren't we almost there?"

Maxim stayed where he was. "Something is wrong. What's going on?"

"We need to keep going," Drake grunted.

"No," Maxim said. "Something is off. We need to head back."

Drake leaned close to Maxim and whispered into his ear. "If you don't continue to move, I will make you regret it."

Maxim glanced back at Drake. The red flashing lights lit up the mysterious American's eyes. They looked dark and full of bloodlust. His legs felt wobbly. He wanted to scream. "Why have I done this? I've doomed my family. I've been foolish. I should have never accepted this!"

Maxim tried to run, but Drake stopped him. He grabbed the psychologist by the shoulder and pinched. He hit a weak spot. Maxim fell to the floor.

"Jason!" Sierra said. "What are you doing?"

"I'm keeping us on task. We need to get to my brother."

Sierra nervously looked up and down the hallway. Due to the red flashing lights, she couldn't see much in any direction. All she knew with any level of certainty was that they were alone.

"Hurry it up," she said to Drake.

Drake picked up Maxim from the floor. The doctor was whimpering and mumbling to himself about how much of an idiot he was.

"You accepted this," Drake said to Maxim. "Now see it through. Get us to my brother."

"The facility is under some sort of distress," Maxim said. "It's probably because of me. They probably know that I've betrayed them. Oksi is going to kill me—"

"Would you shut the hell up?" Drake said. "They don't know anything. It's probably just a power outage. If you freak out right now, they'll suspect you even more when the power comes back on. We need to keep going. These facilities all have backup generators. I give it five to ten minutes before they get it up and running."

"You need to listen to Jason," Sierra said to Maxim.

Maxim wiped the tears from his eyes. He thought about running. But he knew that if he ran, he'd be intercepted by Ukrainian officials, and they'd have questions. He'd be questioned, and they'd connect the dots. They'd discover that he'd snuck foreign agents into the building. His mind raced with worry. He fell to his knees. The panic inside him swelled to a point that was overwhelming.

"Come on," Drake said.

"I can't," Maxim said.

Despite Maxim's small frame, he was as heavy as a bag of bricks. Some facility personnel were running down the hall. Drake let go of the doctor. The personnel rushed past them.

"Jason," Sierra said. "Something's wrong. Look at my phone. It won't work."

"What?" Drake asked.

Another group of facility personnel were making their way down the hall. One of them stopped and talked to Maxim.

"What's going on?" Maxim said.

"I was going to ask you," the man said. "Every piece of electronics in the facility is fried. We're investigating it right now—but it's taking forever. It's like the building was struck by a bolt of lightning. Sorry, but I have to go. We're making sure the cells are all locked."

"We're here to interrogate someone," Maxim said. "The smuggler."

"I don't think we're going ahead with any interrogations right now," the man said. "I suggest you leave. Come back to tomorrow."

The man left.

Maxim turned to Drake. "See? I told you. Something is wrong. Something is very wrong."

"I think we should leave," Sierra said. "We won't get very far like this."

"We can't leave," Drake said.

"What do you mean?" Maxim said.

"I mean, you're going to take us to Colin."

"You heard what the man said," Sierra said.

"It will be worse tomorrow," Drake said. "If the facility is under attack, security protocols will be tightened. It's now or never. And deep down, I have a suspicion this all has something to do with our smuggler."

Sierra nodded and turned to Maxim. "Can you get us into the cell?"

Maxim nodded. "This is stupid, though," he said.

"Just take us to the cell," Drake said.

They ran through the hallways of the facility and found the area with the holding cells mostly empty.

"The holding cell is up here," Maxim said. "Once we get him out, we'll move him to an interrogation cell. I don't know what you want, but that's all I can do. If you can't get him to talk, then you're out of luck."

"I'll get him to talk," Drake muttered. "I have a lot of questions."

THIRTY-SEVEN

In the holding cell, Colin knew something was wrong. The darkness, the alarms, the shouts—he stood up. He knew what was coming. He didn't want to admit it, but he knew. The men who'd hired him had come to clean up their mess.

The door to his cell opened. He hadn't seen natural light in days, and the sudden influx of light made him wince. It was painful.

"Who's there?" he said in Ukrainian.

"He looks just like you," a woman said.

Colin tried to focus, but his eyes still hurt. He was unsure what was going on. All he could see through his adjusting eyes were the shapes of three figures. One of them was tall.

"Grab him and pull him out of there," a man said.

"We can take him to the interrogation room," Maxim said.

"What is this?" Colin said. "Who are you?"

Maxim didn't respond.

Unable to adjust to the light in time, Colin was pulled from the room. The tall man grabbed hold of his arms and lifted him from the floor.

"Who are you?" His eyes began to focus, and the dark and light shapes were beginning to become clear. "Jason?"

Drake pulled his brother out of the cell and down the hallway.

"In here," Maxim said.

"The door is locked," Sierra said.

"I have a key."

Colin shook his head. Had he died? he thought. Was the man beside him really his brother?

"Come on," Maxim said, holding the door open. "Quickly."

Colin was forced into the room.

Maxim locked the door behind him. "We'll be safe here," he said. "But we don't have long."

Colin was forced down onto a chair. He looked up at his brother. His skin turned white. His mouth opened in horror.

"Jason ... is that really you?"

THIRTY-EIGHT

Colin's eyes squinted, still adjusting to the light. He looked up at his brother with a frightened expression.

Jason Drake stared at his brother and didn't respond. He had always prided himself in his ability to push past his emotions but seeing the brother he thought dead alive hit him hard—more than he'd expected. He wanted to be cold, but he couldn't. Instead, he stared at his brother, flooded by an overwhelming sense of personal history, memories that felt more like nightmares.

How many nights had he spent trying to bury the memories of his brother? It was the thought of his loss that had started everything. But now, now he was alive. Was all of that pain, that anguish, for nothing?

One light hung up in the middle of the small holding cell. "Brother, what's going on?"

Drake remained reticent. He examined the man who shared his blood. Colin looked like he'd been through hell. He had thick lines on his thin face. His hair was long and greasy and slicked back. Drake noticed his arms were covered in a sleeve of tattoos. The only give-away that he was Colin was his eyes.

Sierra and Maxim stood at the door. "Jason, we don't have long," Sierra said.

"I know," Drake said.

Sierra turned to Maxim. "Can you watch the halls?"

Maxim nodded. He gave Drake a worried look. He didn't need to be a world-class psychologist to know there was an anger percolating under his skin, one that he was deeply afraid of. He turned to Sierra. "Make sure he doesn't hurt him."

"He's my brother," Drake said. "I won't hurt him."

"You know I don't believe you," Maxim said. "I know how brothers treat each other."

Drake clenched his jaw.

THIRTY-NINE

Colin's eyes had finally adjusted to the light. He looked up at his brother and smiled. "You look good, little brother."

"And you're alive," Drake said, sitting down. Only a table separated the two of them.

"I am for now."

"What does that mean?"

"It doesn't matter what it means. Why are you here? How the hell did you know I was here? And how the hell did you get inside?"

"I came here to talk to you."

"Is that it?"

"Yes."

"Well, how did you know I was here?"

"You said my name during Dr. Rachman's interrogation. My name is... well, my name is flagged. The CIA intercepted Dr. Rachman's communication with the Ukrainian military general who runs this facility. It set alarm bells ringing back at Langley."

"The CIA? Why do they have your name flagged?"

"It doesn't matter."

Colin shook his head. "Look, I know you probably have a lot of questions, but you need to get out of here. Your life is at risk. The men..." Colin stopped himself. "You need to realize that there are certain individuals who want me dead, and, well, I deserve it. They won't stop. You saw those red flashing lights in the hallway? They're coming for me."

"Who wants you dead?"

"Do you honestly think I'm going to tell you that? I'm in one of the most secure places in the world, and I don't feel safe. Anyone can get in here if they have the will. Look, I'm glad you look well, but this reunion ... this should never have happened. You need to leave."

Drake looked at his brother carefully. "I'm not leaving until you tell me who hired you to deliver those chemical weapons," he said.

"Screw you, brother—and I say that with all the goodness in my heart. You need to get the hell out of here," Colin said.

"No," Drake said.

"They're coming for me. I know they are."

The urgency in his voice. The panic. Drake had no reason to doubt the veracity of Colin's worry, but he also had no reason to trust the man who he'd believed dead for almost twenty years.

"You need to tell me who you work for."

"Or what?"

"Or this whole region will explode into war. The CIA believes Russia is planning something."

"And what does that matter to me, Jason? Do you think I care? I'm a smuggler."

Drake grew agitated. He wanted to lash out at his brother. He wanted to threaten him. He was at once angry and overwhelmed with sorrow. It was an unsettling feeling.

Colin sensed his brother's inner turmoil and started to laugh.

There it was, Drake thought. The cockiness, the laissez-faire attitude of Colin's youth. "You were always high-strung," Colin said. "You need to know when to call it a day, bro. This isn't your fight. You need to leave."

"I'm not trying to make it my fight," Drake said. "I'm just trying to make sure my brother's actions don't result in the deaths of millions."

"Stop being so dramatic."

"I've cleaned up your shit my whole life," Drake said. "After you left, it was hell."

"I had to run away."

"And you left me alone. The military officers who showed up at Mom's house twenty years ago had your death certificate. You died in the Iraq War."

"I did ... well, kinda. At least, on paper, I did. Now, listen. You work for the CIA by all indications. I saw the girl at the door. She's beautiful. How about you do yourself a favor and just forget that I'm alive. Just pretend that I'm dead. Go about your perfect life."

"You think my life's perfect? Did you not listen to me? You left me to clean up the mess you created."

Colin stared defiantly at his brother and didn't respond.

"That's right," Drake said. "Remain quiet. Run from responsibility. Be a coward."

"Coward? I ended up in the military! My friends, close friends, died from an Iraqi insurgent IED. If not for a local's help, I would be dead. A farmer pulled out the shards of shrapnel that were embedded in my leg. He saved my life. It was after that, I began to question everything. I didn't want any part of that life. Seeing you as some government shill, some ghost for the CIA, is disappointing, little brother. Clearly, Mother raised you wrong. And that asshole Dave ..." Colin looked away. His thin face seemed skeletal in the darkness, shadows contouring his face in sharp angles.

"Mom's dead," Drake said. "So is Dave."

Colin looked back at Drake and shook his head. "You gotta know I had my reasons for running."

"I don't care what your reasons were."

"I'm sorry," Colin said.

"I don't care about your apologies," Drake said. "I just came here to stop a war. That's it."

"So, you are CIA?"

"I was. This is pro bono—off the record. My connections at the agency brought me here."

"This changes nothing, Jason. You need to leave. I can't tell you a thing. I am sorry for what you had to go through. I'm sorry for the pain I caused—"

Drake cut his brother off. He stood up angrily. "You're going to tell me who hired you to ship those weapons, or I'll—"

Suddenly, loud explosions echoed through the room. Gunshots?

Sierra turned to Maxim. He had a panicked expression on his face. "Jason, we need to run. Someone is shooting at the guards."

Colin laughed. "I told you, brother. That power outage was what I feared. You should leave. I'm dead. Follow your CIA friends and get the hell out of here."

FORTY

Drake looked out of the interrogation room, leaving Colin at the table. Colin didn't care. He just hoped that his brother had finally come to his senses. He hoped that the sounds of gunfire had made it clear that there was no rescuing him.

"Any ID on the shooter?" Drake asked Sierra.

"I don't know," she said.

"Piece of shit," Drake grunted. He glared back at his brother, who was smiling. "I think that asshole wants to die."

The pulsating emergency lights created a strobe effect. Maxim was cowering in the corner of the room. Drake walked up to him and asked, "How do we get out of here? Where's the nearest exit?"

Maxim didn't respond. He looked up at Drake. He seemed stricken with terror. A psychologist who'd finally let the demons he'd dissected from others take over.

Drake picked the weakened psychiatrist up. He held him against the wall. "Where is the nearest exit?"

"What do you mean?" Maxim asked, shaking. Drake thought he could smell urine.

"We need to get the hell out of here," Drake said. "Someone or some force is trying to get to us. We need to move."

"I don't know ..." Maxim whimpered. "I'm not a soldier. I never wanted this."

Drake sneered. "I don't care what you wanted. This is what you got. You drugged up unwilling participants for years—you broke them in their most vulnerable states. You need to understand that if we don't get out of here, the information that my brother holds dies with him. Understand?"

The shots that had sounded far away became louder. Whoever was moving in on their target.

"There's a service stairwell," Maxim said. "It's at the end of the hallway. It goes all the way down to the garage. Here, take my keys and pass. Just leave me here. I deserve this. I deserve to die. I've done horrible things. I betrayed my profession. If you are who you say you are, you'll have everything you need."

"Are there any weapons in this room?" Drake asked.

"No," Maxim said. "I think I saw a dead guard in the hallway. He was holding a rifle."

More shots rang out. They sounded like thunder, like lightning had just struck the very spot Drake was standing on.

Drake crept out of the holding cell. The shooter was in the holding cells, going from room to room—he was looking for someone.

Drake crawled to the downed guard. He checked the poor bastard's pulse. He was dead. Drake had been in front of men in his state hundreds of times in his life. Like calloused fingers that played the guitar, he'd grown accustomed to the pain. He pushed past it. He coldly picked up the rifle the dead officer was holding and grabbed any ammunition he had on him.

He stood up, walking past Sierra and Maxim. He went back into the interrogation room.

"What are you doing?" Sierra asked.

Drake turned to her and said, "I'm getting us out of here. This place is a death trap. Whoever is attacking this place has the advantage. We need to run."

Colin's face intermittently lit up in shades of black and red. He hung his head low. The sirens bellowed, and the shooting outside the hallway grew louder.

"You're coming with me," Drake said.

"I told you," Colin said. "I told you they would come for me. I told the Ukrainians, too! You can't win!"

"Stand up. You're coming with us."

"I want to die. I have my reasons."

"And I have my reasons for saving your sorry ass."

Colin stood up and looked at his brother. "We won't make it out," he said. "This is stupid. I'm not going with you." He swung at Drake, attempting to knock his brother out.

Drake avoided the swing. He then said the same thing that Colin had told him the night he'd abandoned him all those years ago when the two of them were in their mom's front yard. "This is good for you, brother."

Colin's expression turned stupid. He didn't know what Drake meant.

Drake used the butt of the rifle he'd picked up from the dead officer and knocked his brother out. He smacked Colin clean across the chin. He bent down and picked up his unconscious brother, draping him over his shoulders. The asshole was heavy.

"Come on," Drake said to Sierra. "Follow me." Before leaving the room, Drake turned to Maxim. "Are you sure you want to stay?"

"Yes," Maxim said. "If the shooter comes in here, I'll try to stall him. It's the least I can do."

Drake shrugged. He didn't care for the doctor.

They were about to leave the room when a man ran down the hall screaming.

"Roman?" Maxim shouted. "What the hell are you doing here?"

Roman turned around and noticed his brother in the room. "I didn't know, brother. I didn't know what he was going to do. He's a killer. He's going to kill us all!"

Drake looked at Maxim and asked, "What's he talking about?"

"Calm down," Maxim said to Roman. "What is going on? What do you mean, you didn't know what he was going to do?"

"I mean ... the assassin ...." Roman said. "I helped him get inside this facility. He told me he would only kill his target, but this ... this is too much. He's killing anyone who stands in his way."

"For fuck's sake," Drake grunted.

"Roman, you fool!" Maxim shouted. "Who is he?"

"I don't know."

Drake looked outside. He saw the assassin's shadow. He knew, if they were going to make a break for it, now was the time. He looked at Sierra and said, "Are you ready?"

"Yes," she said.

"When we leave this room, just keep running. Don't stop until we get in that stairwell."

Drake jumped out of the hallway first. His brother still on his back, he aimed down the rifle down the hallway toward the shooting. Sierra ran to the stairwell.

Drake saw the silhouette of the shooter at the far end of the hallway and fired. The shooter ducked away for cover.

Drake slowly made his way to Sierra, who held open the door. He fired short bursts anytime he thought he saw even a faint hint of movement.

Maxim and Roman stayed in the observation room. The two brothers were about to come face to face with their past.

FORTY-ONE

Maxim and Roman looked at each other and sighed. The world around them flickered between darkness and red light. Sirens wailed. Both of them felt they'd done wrong in the world.

The shooting out in the hallway crescendoed into a roar—Maxim figured because of Drake, Sierra, and Colin. He figured they were shooting back at whoever was coming for them. He was sure they'd get away. Drake, unlike anyone he'd met, was capable and skilled. Drake was going to be okay. He could feel it, though he couldn't quite explain that feeling.

When the sound of gunfire subdued, Maxim turned to his brother and said, "What is going on? Who is this assassin?"

"My old life has come to haunt me. The Chevka gang—they're connected to some organization that wanted access to this facility. The man—the assassin—he wanted to kill someone you had in here."

"What do you mean, your old life?"

"I mean that I owed money to the wrong people, and even though I paid them, they wanted more. You knew I was a gambler. It's all come back to haunt me. I paid them, but they wouldn't let me go. I had no choice but to help him. I helped him to protect you."

"Who is he?"

"He's an assassin," Roman said. "He's Russian. He wants to

silence the man you have in here. The one you were interrogating. The one you told me about. The smuggler."

"The one the two Americans just snuck out?"

In the confusion of the moment, Roman hadn't considered that the individual who'd carried a man on his shoulders was connected. He chuckled. "I guess so," he said. "This is my fault, brother."

"No," Maxim said. "It's mine. I should never have taken this job. The military offered me so much. I had no choice. I'm the bad man. I shouldn't have brought you here."

"Don't be foolish," Roman said. "You were taking care of your family."

The two men laughed. It was the first laugh they'd shared since their childhood. It felt good. Peaceful, almost, despite the flashing lights and roaring sirens.

An eerie silence fell over the hallway outside. The only sounds they could hear were sirens and footsteps—they were heavy, determined.

"He's coming," Roman said to his brother. "You should hide. He will kill you."

"And what will you do?"

"I'll show you that I'm not the man you think I am. Yes, I'm a gambler. Yes, I'm a piece of shit. But I love you. Hide. I will take care of him."

Maxim looked at his brother with a worried expression. The sense of goodbye flooded the room. They both knew the answer. They both knew that this short but swift meeting was the last they'd speak to each other.

Maxim didn't have time to come to terms with it. He didn't have time to consider all the repercussions. The worry of the attack on the facility had relegated him into a more primitive state—all that mattered was survival. All that mattered was the thought of holding his daughter again. He'd been a bad father. He'd ignored her and his wife. He'd put too many things ahead of them. He promised himself that if he got out of here alive, he'd never take any of that for granted again. He'd never put himself in a position like this again—he'd never go against his Hippocratic oath to help those in need. He wouldn't let his research be used against those who were vulnerable.

He was finally beginning to fully understand the psyches of the men he'd been interviewing, the men he'd drugged to the point of sad interrogation—they all carried with them regret. He had empathy for them. The privileged life he'd lived up to that point had become obvious. The lies he'd told himself to keep going evaporated.

Maxim moved into a darkened corner of the interrogation room. He was invisible.

Roman stood at the door.

The shooter kicked open the door.

———

"YOU WERE SUPPOSED to wait in the holding cells," Artem said. "What the hell are you doing in here?"

"The man you're looking for. He wasn't in his cell. I grew scared."

"You idiot," Artem said. "Where is the prisoner? Have you seen him?"

Roman shook his head. He stared at Artem, and for the first time since meeting the man, he saw a hint of weakness.

Artem heaved, his breaths labored. He stared back at Roman and lifted a rifle he'd picked up from a dead guard.

Roman closed his eyes.

From the shadows, Maxim watched.

"Did you help them get away?" Artem asked Roman—the barrel of his gun aimed square at Roman's chest.

"I did."

"Oh well," Artem said. "I was going to kill you anyway."

"But you said—"

"You were my getaway, fool. Why do you think I am dressed like you? I was going to make it look like the attacker was killed in the onslaught, but only if I got my target, which clearly, I don't."

"You're a monster."

"I'm an assassin," Artem said. "And you are a weak man. Goodbye."

Roman tried rushing Artem, knowing what was going to come next, but before he could get to the assassin, Artem put three holes into Roman's chest. He fell to the floor. His head twisted, his body twitched and convulsed.

In the shadows, Maxim saw his brother fall. He saw blood leak out of the wounds in his chest. He tried to scream, but he had no air in his lungs. It felt like he'd been shot. Roman's lifeless eyes stared at Maxim.

Artem, oblivious to Maxim's presence, knelt down and carefully placed his rifle in Roman's dead hands. He then placed the pistol he'd used to kill the guard in the booth in Roman's pocket.

"They'll think you're the shooter," Artem said. "You'll get all the credit for this mess. It's too bad."

Maxim stayed in the dark until Artem left. When he was sure the assassin was gone, he crept out of the shadows and cradled his brother—who by that point was dead.

FORTY-TWO

Drake left the rifle in the stairwell and carried Colin into the garage. Sierra ran to Maxim's vehicle and opened the doors. Drake placed his unconscious brother in the back seat. Colin moaned; he was waking up.

"Do you want to drive?" Sierra asked Drake.

"Sure."

She tossed him Maxim's keys. He got into the driver's side and started up the engine. She got into the front passenger's seat.

The parking garage was full of security personnel. They were all running inside the complex. The red emergency lights were still flashing.

Drake pulled out of the parking spot slowly. He nodded at the facility personnel and drove out of the garage.

Outside was even more of a mess. Emergency lights and sirens were all on. Ambulances and police cars lined the streets just beyond the iron walls of the facility.

"How are we going to get through this?" Sierra asked Drake. "The cops at the gate. They won't let us out."

"We have an injured man in the back seat," Drake said. "He's unconscious."

Sierra looked back at Colin. His eyes were open, and his nose was bloody. He had a confused expression on his face. He wasn't fully conscious yet, but he was close. "He's waking up."

Drake pulled the vehicle to a stop and looked back at his brother. "Colin? You up?"

"I ... Where am I?"

"Come here," Drake said to Colin. "I'll tell you where you are."

Colin pushed himself up from the back seat. A thick pool of blood stained the cushions his head had rested on. He leaned close to his brother. His pupils were still dilated. "Where am I?" Colin asked. "Is that you, Jason? Jesus ... did you knock me out?"

Drake elbowed Colin in the temple. Colin fell backward, his head tilting to the side, his mouth open.

"What the hell?" Sierra shouted.

"We need him unconscious," Drake said. "It will sell our story. If he's up, they'll bring him to one of the ambulances.

"What story?"

"It's how we're going to get out of this mess," he said. "We'll pull up to the front gates and tell them we have an injured man in the back seat. We still have the credentials, the keys they gave us to enter. We'll just say we're taking *him* to the hospital."

Sierra nodded—she knew it was the only way. Drake drove up to the entrance of the facility. Four military personnel stood at the gate. Two police cruisers were parked on the other side. The police were cordoning off the street. They were trying to lock the place down. She noticed a body being pulled out of the booth outside the facility's front gate.

Drake rolled his window down and looked at the military officer at the exit.

"Who are you?" the officer said. "We need to see your ID?"

Drake responded in Ukrainian. "I have an injured man. We need to get him to the hospital."

"I need to see your papers."

"I have special authorization from General Oksi," Drake said. He handed the officer the same yellow paper Maxim had used to gain access earlier. If the officer took the time to check the paper, there'd be trouble. Drake was hoping that in all the chaos, the officer would be unsettled.

The young officer looked at the paper quickly. All he was looking for was the General's name. Once he saw it, he handed the paper back to Drake.

"We need to get this man out of here," Drake said. "He's unconscious. He needs medical attention."

Sierra marveled at Drake's ability to put on a performance. He sounded like a man desperate, scared. He had an urgency to his voice and let a breathiness linger after he finished a sentence—he sounded sincere, out of breath. He didn't sound at all like the calm and collected man she knew he was. But Drake needed the officer to let them through. He needed the officer not to ask any more questions.

Fire engines and more ambulances pulled up outside the facility. A heavily armed SWAT team rushed into the building. Drake knew the officer manning the gates was scared.

"Listen," he said. "I have special authorization. You saw the paper. There are people who need to get into the facility. There are men down in there. Let me through, and they'll be able to get in. Come on!"

The officer shook his head. He was overwhelmed. He turned to the man operating the booth that controlled the gate and signaled him to open it.

"Get him to the hospital," the officer said.

"You're a good man," Drake said.

The gate opened and Drake drove out.

He pulled around a swarm of police vehicles, their sirens blaring, their lights blazing.

Drake kept his eye on the officer at the gate as it closed behind him. The officer was doubting his decision. He was smarter than he looked. The kid looked like he was going to call the police over and get them to stop Drake.

That was when the janitor shed exploded. Brick and concrete shot up into the air, bits and pieces of the buildings front facade fell, windows shattered. The group of police officers running into the building fell to their knees.

The officer at the gate forgot about Drake.

Drake slammed on the gas and drove down the street.

"Where are we going?" Sierra said.

"I don't know yet," Drake said. He leered back at his brother, whose body rolled and swayed with every sharp turn Drake made. "All I know is we need to get away."

FORTY-THREE

The bomb Artem had placed in the janitor's shed exploded. His plan was working, but only so far. He hadn't completed his primary objective. Still, his target was gone and he needed to get out of there. Whoever had his target was probably already past the front gates. The operation's parameters had shifted completely. It wasn't just the facility he'd be searching for the target now. It would be all of Kyiv—maybe all of Europe.

It'd been too long since he'd been properly challenged. He almost smiled as he left the room. He looked at the the dead janitor on the floor and smiled as he closed the door.

He made his way to the stairwell and looked out of an open window. A swarm of military personnel and police officers were running into the building.

The operation was supposed to be clean. He'd get the janitor to build a small EMP inside the facility's lower levels over a period of several days. Once that was complete, the operation would be a go. The facility would be an open target, vulnerable. Once inside, Artem would shoot his way through a variety of security checkpoints until he found the target: the smuggler. He'd then kill the janitor, frame him by putting the weapon in his hand, and leave the facility in chaos following the second explosion. He'd strip out of the janitorial clothes

and walk out of the facility with nary a scratch. When he was planning it, it almost seemed too easy. He had worried he was getting too
good at his job and that he'd find no satisfaction in it.

But now he had a challenge. He'd have to hunt the bastard down.

In the stairwell, he stripped out of his janitorial clothes, tossed
them inside a trash bin, and made his way to the ground floor.

A facility guard stopped him when he was about to exit the main
building. "Who are you?" he said.

"I work in the holding cells," Artem said, his voice wavering and
panicked. "I heard the shooting and I ran."

The guard looked him up and down. Artem didn't look like a
threat. He looked like a man who belonged in a university. They
didn't suspect him—they were looking for the janitor. They let him
go. Early reports from where the shooting started said the shooter was
in overalls.

Artem made his way outside and walked with a sense of urgency
toward the front gate. As the only way out of the facility, he figured
that whoever had the smuggler had had to pass through the same
gate.

He ran up to the officer manning the gate. He spoke in perfect
Ukrainian. "My friend," Artem said, faking being out of breath. "My
associates, they just left with an injured man—"

The officer cut him off. "They left just before the bomb. They
said they were taking him to the hospital."

"Which vehicle did they take? Mine is still in the garage. I was
supposed to meet with them. When I call the hospitals, I want to
make sure they know which vehicle to identify in their parking lots."

"It was a blue BMW 5 series."

"Thank you." Artem stepped on the gas, but the officer raised his
weapon. He stopped. "What is it?"

"I can't let you out without paperwork."

"I just told you I am looking for my co-workers, associates."

"Can I see your credentials? Paperwork?"

Artem shrugged. He'd been prepared for this, but he hadn't
expected to be in such a rush. His initial escape plan was supposed to
be much more relaxed. He fumbled though his backpack, looking for

the paperwork the Company had prepared for him. Finally, he found it. He'd lost precious seconds. He handed the officer the paperwork.

"Thank you," the officer said.

"Fuck you," Artem said under his breath as he drove through the gates.

FORTY-FOUR

"Roman, Roman!" Maxim sobbed and held his brother in his lap. Tears streamed down his face, his brother's blood soaking his pants. "I'm sorry for what they've done to you, brother!" He kissed his brother's forehead.

Roman's eyes were frozen open. He'd given up his life to protect Maxim. He'd died a hero, although he'd never lived as one.

Maxim was torn inside. His brother had betrayed him by bringing the assassin into the facility. His brother had done so much wrong in his life. Yet, his final act was one of ultimate sacrifice. He'd ensured that Drake, Sierra, and the smuggler would get away.

Maxim felt overwhelmed by emotions he couldn't quite control or fully understand—emotions that would take him years to fully come to terms with. For so long, he'd wanted his brother out of his life. He'd wanted nothing to do with him. How many nights had he told his wife that he wanted Roman to just stay away?

And now, all those thoughts, all those memories, swelled inside. There was a pain inside, in his stomach, that was both a sinking feeling and one of pressure.

Maxim had helped raise Roman after the death of their mother. As much as Roman had become a gambler, a man drawn to corruptness, Maxim knew that he was partly responsible for what he became. Maxim had spent too much time on his studies, his nose buried in books.

"I should have been there for you, brother," he said. "I'm sorry. I'm so sorry."

His brother lay across his lap and he didn't look up when he heard voices outside the interrogation room. They turned to shouts. Their footsteps were loud.

"The bodies!" Maxim heard one of them say.

"They're everywhere."

"This is a massacre."

Two men burst into the room, holding up rifles and flashlights. They were dressed in full body armor. It looked like they were expecting an army.

"Hands up!" one of them shouted to Maxim. "Put him down!"

Maxim did what they told him to do. He let go of his brother, and, sat on the floor, he pushed himself away. His hands slid along the pools of blood.

More armored men ran into the room. A couple of them ran up to Roman and checked his vitals. "The shooter is down," one of them said into their headsets. "I repeat, the shooter is down."

"He's not the shooter," Maxim said.

As quickly as he'd responded, one of the armed men lifted his rifle and aimed it at Maxim. "What did you say?" they said.

"He's not the shooter," Maxim shouted. "The shooter killed him."

"We have reports the man who stormed this complex was a janitor. We have only one registered to work today. And he's dead." The armored officer looked around the room. "And there's the weapon. He stole that rifle from an officer he killed on the lower levels."

"I'm telling you the truth," Maxim said. "I'm a doctor. I come here regularly."

"Your credentials?" the officer said.

"I'm a professor."

"Where's your security clearance? You should have one?"

"I ..." Maxim went for it in his pocket, and then realized where it was. "I don't have it." He realized that Drake and Sierra had taken it. He'd given it to them along with his keys when they left.

The officer he was speaking to grew angry. "What do you mean?"

"I mean, you can look me up. Talk to General Oksi. He knows I'm here. He knows I was meeting the man in this holding cell."

"Put your hands up," the officer said. "Don't move."

"What? You can't be serious!"

"You heard what I said."

"This janitor, this man you accused of being the shooter is my brother. I am telling you the truth and you're not listening. You're wasting your time. The assassin ... the one who killed all those men out in the halls. He has fled the room. You need to go get him. You're wasting your time."

FORTY-FIVE

Drake pulled off the street and parked between a Ford Focus and a Mazda 3, and took a deep breath. They were about ten minutes from the facility. He'd been running on autopilot for the last forty minutes —surviving on trained response and instinct alone. He needed to think and clear his head. He looked back at his unconscious brother and sighed.

"What are you doing?" Sierra asked.

"It's only a matter of time before they find Dr. Rachman," Drake said. "They'll realize he's missing his identification. They'll realize his vehicle is gone. We need to find another method of transportation. They'll come looking for us. The whole country will be looking for this vehicle."

"Where are we going to find another vehicle?"

"Here."

Sierra looked out of the car. "That's stupid, there's too many people. The streets are cluttered."

"Just wait."

He got out of the BMW. The sounds of sirens echoed in the air. Ambulances and police cruisers raced down Esplanada Street. A light rain had started to fall. He looked around the wide open space. A nearby shopping center bustled with foot traffic.

Drake walked alongside the cars, peeking into them. They needed another vehicle and quick. He was hoping someone had left a door unlocked and their keys inside, but there was no such luck.

The only saving grace was that most of the people on the street were distracted, either looking at their phones or the television screens inside bars and cafes—everyone was glued to the news. No one could believe that only a couple of blocks away there was a massive attack on a government-operated facility.

There was a man unloading vegetables from his truck and taking them into a little grocery store at the far end of the street. His truck was parked by a narrow alley.

Drake knew what he had to do.

"Where are you going?" Sierra yelled at him after stepping out of the BMW. "We need to leave. We can't stay here."

"Just wait in the car," Drake growled.

"This is stupid!"

Drake shook his head and waved his hands at her.

Frustrated, Sierra got back in the car.

Drake approached the man unloading vegetables from his truck. He looked like a farmer, probably grew the vegetables on his property and brought them to the city to sell. He wore blue jean overalls and had a white beard.

"Can you help me, sir?" Drake asked in Ukrainian.

The man lowered a box of potatoes to the ground and looked at Drake suspiciously. "What do you want?"

"I'm a little lost."

"Someone in the store can help," the man grunted. "I'm busy."

Drake walked up to the men, stuck his hands in his pockets, and feigned a gun in his jacket by pointing his index finger straight. "I need your help."

The man noticed what Drake was doing. "I should yell for help."

"The police are distracted," Drake said. "No one will care. You'll be dead before they arrive, before anyone can stop me. Don't be stupid. Do what I say."

"What do you want?"

"I want you to walk with me."

"I don't have any money. I'm a poor farmer."

"Go down the alley and walk naturally."

The farmer did what he was told.

"Give me your keys," Drake said.

"What?"

Drake looked left and right. No one had noticed a thing. The two men were standing close to a dumpster. If someone did see them, they probably thought some drug deal was taking place and didn't want to worry themselves with the knowledge.

"Give me the keys to your truck," Drake said.

"But I need it... I'm a poor—"

Drake did what he had to do. He didn't like doing it—the farmer was just doing his job, but there was no time to argue. He knocked the old farmer unconscious and dragged his body behind the nearest dumpster. Drake opened his wallet and stuffed five hundred euros into the man's front pocket.

"I'm sorry," he said.

He then searched the man's overalls and found his keys.

He quickly walked back to the truck, closed up the back cab and pulled up beside the BMW. He jumped out, leaving the truck running, and opened the backdoor of the BMW. His brother was up.

Drake looked at Sierra. "You okay?"

"He's still groggy," she said.

Drake turned to Colin, ""You good to walk?"

"You son of a bitch!" Colin grunted.

"If you want to die, you'll stay here," Drake said. "Unless, of course, you want to end up back in a Ukrainian prison."

Colin rubbed his head and slowly pushed himself out of the backseat. "This is so messed up," he said. He got out of the BMW and stepped into the truck. Before sitting down, he turned to his brother and asked, "Who the fuck are you?"

"Just get in," Drake said.

Colin shook his head and continued to rub his head.

"Are you coming?" Drake yelled at Sierra. She was still in the front seat of the BMW. "If you stay here, you'll regret it."

"I'm sorry," she said. "I just need a second."

"You've had it. Now we need to go."

She hopped out of the BMW and got inside the truck.

Drake tossed the keys to the BMW onto the ground and joined them inside the truck.

"What the hell is going on?" Colin said. "Who the hell are you, man?"

"I should be asking you that," Drake muttered. "You're the one who won't talk. You're the one who's supposed to be dead. Who was that assassin?"

"You should have left me there. I wanted to die. I knew the assassin was coming for me. You don't know who you're messing with."

"Just shut up," Drake said. "Stay quiet."

"Where are we going?" Sierra asked.

"I don't know," Drake said. "We need to travel in this vehicle for a couple of hours. At least until the farmer I just knocked out wakes up. We just need to move."

"I know a place where we can go," Colin said.

"What?" Drake said.

"I'm a smuggler," Colin said. "I know this area well. I know a place we can stay. It's a broken-down house out in the middle of the woods. Just drive east—I'll guide you."

FORTY-SIX

Price stared at her computer monitor. Her eyes felt dry and she was tired. It was one of her final days in office. She'd spent the last few days looking over the past experiences of executives and directors within Langley—President Clarkson wanted the transition to be seamless. Price recommended she give him a list of names that he could then create a task force with. It was the least she could do.

She wanted to find a team that was not just capable, but who weren't going to put themselves and their careers above the job.

It gave her time to consider the last few CIA Directors. They'd had their faults; she was included in this list.

She knew what her faults were.

She never wanted the job. She knew that it was too political; that it required too many meetings. She hated that about it. While she had been a spy for the agency for years, life out in the field was different than life in an office. She had an objective while in the field —she had a goal. The only thing stopping her from completing it were the bad guys—the ones who wanted to see America fall. It was different as Director. The bad guys weren't as clear. There were too many people simply out for themselves. The line between good and evil, right and wrong, seemed blurrier than ever as Director. It didn't help that she had trouble making friends.

The Director before her had been one of those fools who let his career objective get in the way of the main objective. Tom Fowler was a man who couldn't get out of his own way. He had a great resume and was talented, but had been corrupted by power and greed.

The Director before him, Cliff Taggart. He was a curmudgeon, but he knew how to play the game. He commandeered power. He didn't seek it, he just wielded it.

Price knew she was more in line with Taggart, but that didn't mean much to anyone else. She didn't command the room the way he had.

She needed out. The agency needed her out.

She continued to read through agency profiles when her phone rang.

"What is it?"

"The news," her secretary said. "You said you wanted an update on anything in Ukraine. Have you seen the news about Kyiv?"

Price hung up and pulled up the internal news site the agency used. It aggregated headlines from around the world into an easy-to-read repository.

"Holy hell," she said. "What the hell is going on?"

The headlines were all the same.

'Bombs in Ukraine Military Building in Kyiv, Dozens Dead'

'Massacre in Ukraine's Temny Facility, Bombs, Numerous Dead.'

She knew that whatever the hell was happening in Kyiv, it had to do with Sierra and maybe Drake. She quickly read through the news reports. Law enforcement and military were hush-hush. The early reports suggested the attacker was dead, but Price didn't buy it. The operation seemed tactical—military. The shooter, according to the reports, was a janitor with ties to the Russian mob. His brother allegedly got him the job at the facility.

Her secretary rang again. "Madame Director, the President is on the phone. He wants to chat."

"Put him through."

Like a virus multiplying inside a host, news was spreading. Price just hoped Sierra was alive and wasn't in the facility. If she was, this was about to get a lot messier.

"This is the White House," a voice said.

"And this is Kate Price, CIA Director."

"Hold for the President ..."

Price nervously waited.

FORTY-SEVEN

They drove for miles and miles. The rain that had started to fall as they left the city had picked up. The dense streets of Kyiv quickly vanished and were replaced with rolling hills and thick forests. As the sun set, a thick fog fell over the landscape. They didn't know where they were headed, but they knew they had to get away—they had to keep pushing.

Drake was listening to a local news radio station. He figured the information released to the public would be limited, but it was better than nothing. He needed to keep tabs on what the press knew, on what the authorities were allowing them to say.

"We do not have a confirmed number of dead," the radio host said in Ukrainian. "The death toll of today's attack currently stands at fifteen. Six more are in the hospital with critical wounds. The main suspect is believed to be dead at the scene ..."

Sierra was trying to read Drake's face to determine the severity of the situation. Since she didn't understand Ukrainian she was lost. She felt anxious and knew that she had to update Price, but also that she had to be careful: people would be listening, and she needed to keep herself separate. She looked at Drake nervously. "What are they saying? Is it bad? Are they looking for us? Did they say anything about the CIA?"

Drake shook his head. "No. They didn't say anything about the CIA. In terms of looking for us—they have nothing yet. But it's only been three hours since the attack. They're still probably putting the pieces together, retracing steps, listening to survivor testimony. It'll be difficult for them. Whoever was trying to kill Colin was a professional. He knew exactly what he was doing. But I imagine it won't take them too long to figure that Maxim is at the center of this. It won't be long before they realize he's somehow connected to this, and they search for his vehicle. I imagine within three or more hours, they'll connect the stolen truck in the market to us."

Colin's eyes were closed, but he was listening. "You speak Ukrainian?"

"I needed to."

"What were you? A spy?"

"I've been many things."

Colin rubbed his head. "How the hell did you end up in this life, brother? I hoped for more for you. Instead, you wallow in the shadows, like me. You were smart. Why didn't you become an engineer or something? You could have had a peaceful life!"

"I had no choice."

"Really?"

"Yes," Drake grunted.

"You're a fool. You could have been so much more. You're just a spook—an international cop—"

Drake cut him off. "And you're just a smuggler who ended up in a Ukrainian military facility."

"You should have left me. And in regards to my smuggling, I did what I had to do. I wasn't smart like you. I'm just a dumb ass."

"Where the hell is the place we're going to?" Drake said, frustrated. "We've been driving for hours, and we need to figure out where to go next. Is this the right road?"

"We're getting close," Colin said. "And you shouldn't complain about anything. You put yourself in this mess. I wanted to die."

"You sound like a coward."

"I'm not a hero. I don't want to save the day. I just want what's best for me and mine. The men who hired me ..." He drifted off and looked out the window at the rolling green hills of the Ukrainian landscape. "The men who hired me are more powerful than you believe. They have expectations of their contractees. I failed. It was a risk I took. But now ..."

"Now what?"

"Now you have put people at risk who shouldn't be. You've complicated things."

"And what about the Russian soldiers the chemical weapons you were going to deliver were going to kill?"

"It's war. They knew what they signed up for."

If Drake wasn't driving, he would have smacked his brother in the mouth again. He thought about pulling over to do it but resisted the urge. Instead, he kept his silence. In a way, he knew his brother was right—he'd become what was expected of him. He'd become the criminal his teachers had always feared he would be.

Sierra remained silent during the conversation. She could sense a strong amount of trauma between the two men. She was growing to understand Drake more—more than perhaps she wanted to. He wasn't just the killer the CIA had recruited into their Terminus division—he was something else.

"Where is the safe house?" Drake muttered.

"At least fifteen minutes away," Colin said. "You'll see a dirt road to the right. It will be in the midst of dense brush—it'll kinda be like the Wallace Farm back home. Do you remember that?"

Drake didn't want to remember. He'd spent years of his life shutting out the memories of his past. But now, seeing Colin ... it became hard not to look back. Dreams and memories he'd thought gone forever rose from the dead like zombies clawing themselves up from a grave. He felt the rotting hands of his past grip his neck and suffocate out the facade of the present. "Wallace Farm had the chickens," he grunted.

Colin chuckled. "You were so young. We'd sneak in there at night. You were probably only six or seven. Dad was still around then. Do you remember the barn? It looked like something out of a horror movie. That's kinda like the place we're going. You'll see a break in the forest just ahead. It won't look like it's drivable, but it is."

Drake nodded. "We used to climb up the rotting wooden panels. I remember looking up at the stars at night."

"We'd grab the eggs," Colin said. "Mom was such a drunk she never questioned why the fridge was always full of fresh eggs."

Drake couldn't help but smile. The memory was a good one. It felt like he was betraying a part of himself, though. He hated looking back. He remained silent for the rest of the car ride.

Fifteen minutes later, a dirt road appeared between a thicket of trees. It was narrow and bumpy. It looked like it wasn't drivable. "This is it?"

"Yes," Colin said.

Branches hung over the road like a gateway, at once inviting and threatening. Drake drove up the road and a couple of minutes later, spotted the safe house. It was in a clearing. It looked like a dilapidated cabin.

"What is this place?"

"It's my safe house," Colin said. "Who knows when it was built. Men like me are sure to have places like this around major cities. I come here when I need to lie low. It has supplies."

"What kind of supplies?"

"Canned food," Colin said. "And alcohol."

Despite his brother's assurances, Drake didn't trust him. He turned off the truck's headlights and came to a stop just before leaving the wooded path and emerging into the clearing. "We go by foot the rest of the way," he said.

"What? Why?" Sierra asked.

"Because I don't trust him," Drake said of Colin. "I want to be careful."

"You always were the cautious one, little brother. But it's the smart thing to do."

Sierra chuckled. "If you think Jason is cautious, what does that make you?"

"Fearless," Colin said.

"It makes you an idiot," Drake corrected. "Colin didn't go one year without breaking a couple of bones."

After pulling the keys out of the ignition, Drake hopped out of the truck. The land around the house was muddy on account of the rain—thankfully, it had stopped. There were now breaks in the sky where the stars could pierce through.

All three walked up to the safe house and went inside.

FORTY-EIGHT

For the first time in a long time, Artem had a challenge. He loved it. The harder the kill, the bigger the reward. His target was still on the run. His assassination had been interrupted by a foreign force. It was now a game of cat and mouse. It was a game Artem was hellbent on winning.

Most of his victims relied on the police or military for protection. Artem knew how to slice through their walls of defense—a disabled security camera and a bribe went a long way. He once killed a man in a prison cell in New York City. A man whose cell was surrounded by guards and was under twenty-four-seven observation.

Whoever had interrupted his assassination was trained—special. Whoever had pulled his target out of the facility was an individual who had earned Artem's respect.

After leaving the Temny Facility, Artem walked through the streets of Kyiv back to his hotel. There was so much chaos surrounding the facility that no one noticed him. He held his head low and disappeared into a wall of cluttered police cruisers and ambulances.

He could feel his heart rate elevate as he walked through the streets to his hotel—he enjoyed the pounding sensation. It reminded him that he was alive.

Once in the hotel, he made his way to his room. After a quick shower and change of clothes, he went to the hotel bar. He needed to calm his nerves and reassess. He knew that President Makarov would be watching the news. He knew the President would know that things had not gone to plan, and he knew that the President would be waiting for an update.

Artem ordered a rye and coke. He texted his contact at the Company, via an encrypted channel, a coded message:

The bird is alive. Still hunting.

The glass of rye and coke he ordered was placed on the bar in front of him. Artem enjoyed his drink while watching the news.

A breaking news banner flashed across the screen.

"This is the latest news on today's awful attacks," the anchor said. "Ukrainian police and military services are still trying to make sense of it all. The man suspected of the attack has now been cleared. We no longer suspect the janitor ...."

Artem tensed. Had he acted too arrogantly? Had he made a misstep? Was he the suspect?

The news anchor continued: "The police have released this image of a stolen vehicle, a red Toyota truck. The persons of interest are believed to have left the city in the truck. If you see it, do not approach. Those inside are believed to be armed and dangerous. A man missing from the facility, a foreign smuggler, is believed to have been taken hostage."

Artem finished his drink in one gulp and ordered another. Things couldn't have been better, he thought. They were literally barking up the wrong tree.

"Good day at the office?" the bartender asked, noticing Artem's smile.

"What do you mean?" he asked.

"The smile on your face. That's all."

Artem chuckled, and his face turned red. "Yes, yes. It was a great day. I am celebrating."

"Where do you work?"

The bartender was blonde and pretty. She had blue eyes, and lush red lips. Artem thought of all the awful things he could do to her. He caught himself, realizing how she might interpret his sudden doziness, his sudden intense focus. He looked away. "I work in sales," he said. "I just ... I just made a big sale."

"What do you sell?"

He sighed. If only they all fell into his web so easily. He leaned in close to the bar and put on his charm. She leaned close to him. He touched her hand and winked at her. Perhaps, he thought, he should have a little fun—a little stress relief before the end of the night. Perhaps he should expel the urge. He'd extinguish her flame. Kill her with little mercy. He grew aroused just thinking about it. He had to shift himself on his stool to hide his arousal. "When do you finish work?" he said.

"In thirty minutes," she said.

"Perfect."

At that point, another breaking news bulletin caught the corner of his eye. The television was hung up over the back wall of the bar, above an assortment of spirits.

"The vehicle was last spotted heading toward the Romanian border."

His excitement faded. He knew he had to leave the hotel.

The blonde bartender stoked Artem's hand. "I can finish earlier," she said. "It's not a busy night."

He turned to her and chuckled. "I apologize," he said. He stood up, leaned in, and whispered in her ear. "You are a lucky girl."

She pulled herself back, confused. "What do you mean?"

"Nothing," he said. He needed to keep his eyes on the prize. He needed to focus. While the urge to kill was there, he needed to act rationally. She'd have to live. If he'd given in to his old patterns, he'd have killed the girl. He wanted to cut her throat and let her blood spray out across the hotel bathroom floor. He had to fight the thought. It was pervasive in his mind, like a drug or toxin.

He needed to leave. If the police were looking for a red truck, it meant he needed to listen to a police radio channel, and there was only one way he was going to gain access to a police radio channel.

He left the hotel bar and walked out of the lobby back onto the street.

He walked away from the hotel. There was no need to check out. Everything he'd brought with him was in his duffel bag. He placed it over his shoulders and walked back toward the Temny Facility. He needed to find a police cruiser.

FORTY-NINE

The safe house had a draft coming through the walls. There was no respite from the natural elements outside. A strong wind cut like a surgeon's knife when it hit your skin. It seemed to get under it— attack the bones. The rain outside had picked up and dripped from the ceiling. It was an uncomfortable place.

"Welcome to paradise," Colin said sarcastically as he walked into the small house. He made his way to a dresser at the far end of the room and opened up a small drawer. He pulled out some matches, and grabbed a candle from atop the dresser, and lit it up. "There are cans of beans under the bed."

"What the hell is this place?" Sierra moaned as she walked in and looked around.

"It's not a five-star hotel, sweetheart," Colin said. "It's a place with a roof, and it's out of the way. I don't know how many times I've had to use this hide-out. The smuggling business is more about laying low than you'd think. I spent a whole summer here once ..." He looked out the window, out into the darkness of the night, lost in a memory. "It was one of the best summers of my life. There's a small creek that flows through the forest. I'd go days without hearing a vehicle down the main road. I was at peace."

Drake looked around the safe house. It was about the size of a big shed. There were no rooms, and the furniture was moldy and covered in black blotches. He walked up to the bed and noticed that some floorboards were loose. That was where Colin had kept the food. He lifted up the floorboard but grunted in frustration when he saw that the cans of beans had been soiled—rats. He turned back to Colin and said, "We need to talk."

"Are the beans any good?"

"No."

"Shit," Colin said. "I haven't had a proper meal in a week."

"A proper meal?" Sierra said. "You think a can of beans is a proper meal?"

Colin shrugged. "I am not a man of luxury. I do what I have to do to survive. I live in the real world, the one filled with those struggling to get by—who hate their nine-to-fives but do it anyway. Those folks, they do what they have to do."

Sierra's eyes narrowed. She stepped toward Colin in a threatening manner. "I grew up on a small farm. You don't know shit about me! I've struggled."

"I know enough," Colin said. "You're a beautiful woman. And because of that, things come easy to you. You don't know loss. You don't know—"

She slapped him across the face.

Colin's cheek turned red.

Drake laughed. "You deserved that."

"She's a bitch!" Colin barked.

Sierra slapped him again.

Colin went to strike back, but Drake grabbed his arm. "You hit her, I'll break your jaw. She's the only reason you're not dead."

Colin wiggled his arm free from Drake's grasp and sat down on the bed. "I wanted to be dead," he moaned.

Figuring the situation was under control, Drake asked his brother, "Who were you protecting? Why did you want to die?"

Colin looked at the floor. In the candlelight, his face looked skeletal. Long and deep shadows exaggerated the contours of his face. "I can't tell you," he said in a sullen way.

"Why?" Drake said. "You can help stop a war between Russia and Ukraine if you tell us the truth. For whatever reason, President Clarkson won't act. We have a feeling it has something to do with you —your shipment."

"Screw you, Jason," Colin said. "Twenty-four hours ago, I was at peace with my life. I knew what I was. Now, you're asking me to do what's right? Are you dumb? I'm a fucking criminal. I've delivered weapons to bad people who've used them to kill good people."

Drake stared at Colin with a direct and stoic expression. He knew it bothered his brother. It bothered most people. The less you gave them, the less they had. And not many people could stand that kind of attention. It made them feel weak, vulnerable. It made them feel unsafe. They'd react. They'd reveal themselves.

"You're an idiot," Colin said. "You can't stop this war. It will happen whether you want it to or not. The best course of action is to just look after yourself."

"You're lucky I didn't run into you sooner," Drake said. "I spent years hunting down men like you. Men who sell chemical weapons to rebel groups—men who exchange death for profit. A long time ago, I would have killed you without thinking twice, brother or not."

"Then you're no saint either, brother. If you think you were doing *good,* you don't know how the world works. Men like me are a dime a dozen. You kill me, it changes nothing. The men who hired me will find someone else. And trust me when I say there is always someone else. You fucked up rescuing me. You think getting me out of that prison will stop anything? You don't know a thing. The men who hired me are well-connected. I don't even know how high it goes, to be honest. All I know is that if you work for them and you get caught, you have to accept your fate. If you don't, they come after your family. That's why we need to head to Istanbul."

"I am family."

"You're not *my* family," Colin said. "You're my past. You're my shadow. Nothing more."

"I'm your brother," Drake said. "You can keep complaining about how I should have left you in that cell, but it won't change a thing.

You're out. You're in my custody. And you're going to tell me what you know. There is no option."

"It's not that easy," Colin said. "You think I'm going to come to terms with my death and then just tell you everything I know? You don't know the series of events you've set in motion by pulling me out of there. I'll tell you what I know in time. In their eyes, I'm sure it looks like this was my plan all along. I'm sure they blame me for my escape, even though I wanted nothing of it. They'll blame the people I love. I'll tell you if you help me."

"What do you need help with?"

"The men who hired me know where I lived. My wife is there. We need to rescue her."

"Where did you live?"

"Istanbul—it's why I brought you here. We're a day's drive away. I know they'll make me an example for anyone else who doesn't comply with their process. I know how they work."

"I could torture you," Drake threatened. "I could squeeze the truth out of you. I don't need to take you to Istanbul."

Colin chuckled. "I may be a dumb coward, but I'm not an idiot. Even the Ukrainians couldn't get me to talk—despite their various efforts. You know that doctor you were with drugged me, right? He put me in a state I've never been in before. I've done about every drug you can do—heroin, LSD—but the stuff he administered while I was in that cell was some of the heaviest shit I've ever done. And despite his worst, I didn't talk. You could break every bone, you could bring me to the cusp of death, and I won't squeal. I have too much on the line, brother. I know you need me. I know you need me or you wouldn't have risked everything to save me. So, don't go all acting stoic. Don't pretend that you think you have control."

Drake turned away from his brother. He knew Colin was right. He sat down on the floor beside Sierra and said to Colin, "So, you're holding all the cards, then? You're in control? I knew it was a waste coming here. When I heard you were the one in the Ukrainian cell, I said 'let him rot.'"

Sierra looked down at Drake. He seemed lost in a maze of his own thoughts. "That's not all you said," she said. "You said that he deserved to know the truth."

"What truth?" Colin asked.

"I'll tell you on our way to Istanbul," Drake said.

"So, you'll help me?"

"I just want to know who you work for. After that, you can disappear and play dead again. After that, I never want to see you."

FIFTY

Drake, Sierra, and Colin left the safe house first thing in the morning. They left before the sun rose. As the sun's light diffused through the branches, Drake took a deep breath. Birds chirped in the trees, and the rustling waters of the nearby stream made the place feel still. He could understand why Colin liked the place, why he'd spent a whole summer there hiding out.

He joined Sierra and Colin in the truck and drove down the small path back to the main road. He drove toward Odessa, a coastal city close to the Romanian border.

Drake listened to the radio as he drove. The various news anchors kept repeating the same thing: the authorities were looking for a red Toyota truck. They said it was connected to the attack on the Temny Facility, though they didn't say how. All they said was that the red truck was key to the attack. They were right, up to a point, Drake thought.

Because of information about the red truck being the target of interest, Drake kept mostly to side roads. Colin's smuggling past helped in this respect—the man knew how to hide, how to lay low. It was his specialty. He knew the backroads of Ukraine as well as any local.

"I've been back and forth on these roads a dozen times," Colin chuckled. "The men I work for had me smuggle everything. I once smuggled a prized llama out of a farm."

"Why were you smuggling a llama?" Sierra asked.

"I don't ask questions," Colin said. "All I can tell you is that thing stunk up the back of my moving truck like you wouldn't believe."

Drake observed Colin carefully. Just two days earlier, he'd thought his brother dead. For years, he'd envisioned his brother as some heroic fighter—someone who'd died in the throes of battle. The military police who'd told his mother about Colin's passing, after all, had said Colin died protecting his team. It gave Drake an impression that didn't seem to match well the reality of the man who was alive and well in the truck. The man in the truck was no hero. He smuggled llamas.

Drake had a million questions. He knew he'd get a chance to discuss with his brother what had happened, eventually. All he had to do was wait for Sierra to leave. When she was gone, they'd talk. Maybe then the truth would come out.

"There's a road up ahead that will help us cross the Romanian border," Colin said. "There's no checkpoint. It's unguarded. Once we cross it, it will be clear sailing until the Turkish border. Once we get there, we need to hit up the Dagesh checkpoint. I know the man who controls it. If we pay him enough, he'll let us across. After that, it'll be clear sailing to Istanbul."

"Pay him?" Sierra asked. "We don't have much cash. They better not ask for much."

"I'm sure we'll figure something out," Colin said, winking at Sierra. "Hell, he might let us in if you promise him a kiss."

Sierra shook her head in disgust. "You won't pimp me out."

Drake spoke up. "Sierra's not coming with us across the border," he said.

"What?" Sierra and Colin said in unison.

"They're looking for this truck," Drake said. "She's going to have to drive it once we hit Romania. She'll drive it west, as far west as she can. Until they stop her."

"I'll be arrested."

"You'll be fine," Drake said.

"Kate wanted to keep the CIA out of this. If the Ukrainian military arrest me, they'll know the CIA are involved. Word will spread. Kate is dealing with enough in DC. You know that."

"We've hit an inflection point," Drake said. "We need to make a major pivot. Kate's a big girl—she'll be able to handle it."

"It's the President, Jason," Sierra said. "His advisors have him convinced that if we get involved with this conflict, war will break out."

"So, we should just let them catch us."

"Why can't I go with you? We'll just park the truck somewhere they won't find it."

"I want them to find it. You need to throw off the scent," Drake said. "You need to buy us time."

"Time?"

Drake looked back at Colin. "If I help you, you'll tell me who you're working for?"

"Yes," Colin said. "But we need to get Istanbul. They'll be going for my wife."

Drake looked briefly at Sierra as he sped down the road. "I help him, he opens this whole thing up. You and Kate both think there's more to this than meets the eye. It's why you're here. It's why she sent you."

"I came here because he mentioned your name."

Colin shook his head. "That asshole doctor drugged me. That's why I said his name."

"And that's why I'm here," Drake said. "Something is up. Something big. Who hired him? Who wanted him dead?"

"I told you who wants me dead," Colin said. "It's part of the contract I have working with these assholes."

"Right," Drake said. "But you were delivering chemical weapons to Crimean pro-Ukrainian rebels. If those rebels had used those weapons on Russian troops, it's conceivable that Russia would have the justification to invade Ukraine. One might even think that was the point. Ukraine would look foolish if those rebels got away with it. Russia would only be protecting itself if it went to war."

"It wasn't the Russians who hired me, brother," Colin said. "I guarantee you that. If you think this is some Russian conspiracy, you're barking up the wrong tree. You sound like a conspiracy theorist. You're drawing too many lines between too many parts."

"I'll get to the bottom of this," Drake said. "There's more here. I know there is. And the only way I'll get to the bottom of it is if Sierra takes this truck."

"If you're wrong, we could be risking a war," she said. "If the President's advisors are right, we could be the cause of a Russian invasion."

"So, the options are: war or war?" Colin quipped.

Drake shook his head. "You're still a piece of shit, you know that?"

"And you're still my little brother. So serious. So concerned about things you can't control."

"Fine," Sierra said. "I'll take the truck."

"I'd honestly prefer if the pretty lady stayed with us," Colin said. "She's a lot nicer than you."

Drake ignored his brother and kept driving down the slow, unpopulated side roads. After three hours of driving, they crossed the Romanian border. Drake drove to a small town about an hour west of the Black Sea's coast called Cremshank.

"This is where we will change vehicles," Drake said, pulling to a stop.

The village was old and squalid, the roads littered with trash, and many of the buildings front facades were chipped or broken.

"Where do we get a vehicle here?" she said.

Drake turned to Colin. "Well? Do you know anyone in this town?"

Colin smiled. "I know a man. He might help us."

"Might?" Drake asked.

"You'll find out why when we meet him. He lives ten minutes out of town. He has a sheep farm."

Drake rolled his eyes and drove to the farm.

FIFTY-ONE

Inside an Odessa internet cafe, Artem logged into an online public chat. The cafe was busy and smelled like a gym locker. Those inside were hunched over their screens, the blue glow shining on their greasy faces. Artem needed to get in contact with the Company. He needed to give them an update.

After paying for thirty minutes of access to a computer in the corner of the room, he logged onto a social media platform that was as big as Facebook and Twitter, though less refined, less controlled. It was how he and the Company communicated

What made the platform helpful was that you could chat about anything you wanted—every communication was private, encrypted.

He got away, Artem typed.

He didn't have to worry about the eyes of those around him. After typing, what he wrote showed up as a series of numbers and symbols on his screen.

I've seen the news, his contact with the Company responded. The message came along as an encrypted code.

It took Artem forty seconds to decipher the numbers and symbols. He had the cipher written on a piece of paper. To say the Company was paranoid would be putting it lightly.

I am tracking them, Artem typed. *Someone, some group, inter-*

fered. I acquired a police cruiser. I hear all their communication chat-
ter. The vehicle they're in is headed to Romania.

Any idea on the group? CIA? Other foreign service?

Nothing yet.

He's most likely heading home.

Where's that?

Istanbul.

They're not supposed to run.

He might think he has a chance to survive. Who knows.

Do you know his address?

Artem wrote down the address the Company sent.

He didn't know who he was speaking to. All he knew was that the information they sent him was accurate.

He left the internet cafe and walked back to the stolen police cruiser.

He started up the vehicle and, before pulling out, listened to the police chatter. There was no update. The red truck was last seen north of Odessa, driving south. He heard a thumping noise come from the back of the vehicle. It was the cop he'd stolen the vehicle from. The bastard had woken up.

He'd kept the cop alive in case any law enforcement officials wanted to hear confirmation that the cop was okay. So far, the cops working at the station in Kyiv hadn't suspected a thing. They seem-ingly didn't even know a cop had been kidnapped—the whole country was in a state of panic. They'd figure it out eventually, however. The cop's family had probably already reported the poor bastard missing.

Artem knew he'd have to dispose of the car and the cop.

He drove thirty minutes out of Odessa and pulled over down a small, wooded path. It looked like a place hikers or photographers would go. It was beautiful. The crashing waves of the Black Sea could be heard in the distance.

Artem opened the trunk and looked at the cop. The young man had petrified eyes. He moaned and flung his arms and legs in all directions. He kicked and screamed like a petulant child. Artem had tied his wrists and ankles together and taped the cop's mouth shut.

He grabbed the cop by the neck, pulled him out of the trunk, and dragged him from the car toward the sound of the waves.

"This was always going to be the way it was going to end," he said in the cop's native Ukrainian. "I'm sorry I found no use for you."

Tears streamed down the cop's face. He tried in vain to free himself from Artem, but he couldn't—the man was too strong.

Artem dragged the howling cop to the edge of the forest. There was a thirty-foot drop to the water below.

After tossing the cop on the ground, Artem pulled out a pistol.

The tape around the cop's mouth loosened from his saliva. "Please!" the young cop screamed. "I have children! I won't tell them a thing. Just let me live ... please, let me live."

Artem was emotionless. He stared at the pleading cop, his body shifting along the edge of the cliff like a worm on sun-dried cement. He lifted the pistol, aimed it at the cop's head, and pulled down on the trigger.

A splatter of blood and bone spilled from the cop's head and soaked into the dirt.

There was no need to bury the body. Artem kicked it into the water. He watched as it splashed and disappeared. He knew the authorities would find it, eventually—it might take them days or weeks. It didn't matter to Artem. By the time they found it, he'd be gone, and he knew that when they did find it, it'd be either too bloated to identify or in pieces. With any luck, some animal—a bear or a wolf preferably—would come across it on the shore and rip it apart. The forensic team would spend another week trying to determine the cause of death.

Artem would be long gone by then. He walked back to the car, got inside, and drove to Turkey, to the address the Company had given him.

He was about to make sure that the smuggler understood he couldn't take matters into his own hands. The smuggler knew the contract. Once caught, he was supposed to die.

Running was never an option.

Never.

FIFTY-TWO

"Long time, no see, Alexandru," Colin said.

Alexandru Balan stood at the doorway of his small farmhouse and stared at Colin. He had a large, round tummy and a thick beard, and he didn't look happy.

"I told you never to come to Cremshank again," Alexandru grunted. His voice was low and sounded like a grizzly.

"It was a misunderstanding," Colin said. "I thought you'd be over it by now."

"You slept with my wife and stole my car. How is that a misunderstanding?"

Drake and Sierra stood behind Colin. Drake rubbed his head and rolled his eyes.

"Is it bad?" Sierra asked Drake.

"He slept with this asshole's wife," he said.

"He did what!? Why will this guy help us?"

Drake didn't need to respond. Alexandru, despite his size, was quick. He punched Colin in the jaw. The older Drake brother fell on his back on the wooden floorboards of the decking. Alexandru then spit on him. "Fuck you!" the Romanian farmer said. He slammed the door to his house shut.

Colin pushed himself up from the floor and turned to Drake. "That went better than expected."

"Better than expected?" Sierra asked. "He looks like he wants to kill you. Jason said you slept with his wife?"

"Yeah, it went better than expected," Colin said, cracking his neck. "I thought he was going to kill me. The fact he didn't means he might still help us."

Colin knocked on the front door again.

Alexandru opened it, ready to swing again, but Colin raised arms in self-defense and said, "Listen, mate, I'm sorry. I did sleep with your wife. But I was very drunk that night—and, well ... your wife, she was kind of a problem. You're lucky to not have her in your life anymore. In a way, I helped you."

"She was a slut," Alexandru said. "After she slept with you, I found out the whole village had basically slept with her."

"You see," Colin said. "I was a fool that night. I'm sorry."

"Do you want a coffee?" the farmer offered.

"I'd love one."

"Who are your friends?" Alexandru asked, noticing Drake and Sierra.

"Long story."

Alexandru shrugged and invited Colin, Drake, and Sierra inside his small home. He'd worked with Colin on and off through the years. The smuggler always had a story—and could never be trusted.

Drake, Colin, and Sierra sat down at his kitchen table. Alexandru boiled some water in a kettle atop his stove. The house felt cold and dark. Outside the windows, sheep grazed in the fields.

"Did you kick her out?" Colin said, sitting down. He plopped his feet up on the table.

"Yes," Alexandru replied. "I kicked her out. She's now living with Anita."

"The librarian?"

"She says she's a lesbian now."

Colin smirked. "I could have told you that," he said. "When I slept with her, Anita was there, too. The two women seemed more interested in each other than me. You wouldn't believe—"

Under the table, Drake kicked his brother's leg.

Colin looked at Drake.

"Cut it out," Drake said under his breath. "You're lucky we've made it this far."

Colin waved his hands, letting Drake know that everything was fine. He turned back to Alexandru, who was still making the coffee. "It's for the better, mate."

"It doesn't matter," the farmer said. "It's in the past—I've moved on. And in all honestly, all I wanted to do was punch you in the face. I didn't like her that much, anyway—she was a terrible cook and never cleaned the house. Even the car you took was a pain my ass. It couldn't have taken you far."

Colin laughed. "It broke down just outside of Budapest. That whole ordeal almost killed me. I spent three weeks in a Croatian police cell nursing a bullet in my calf. They let me go after I told the police chief how much the llama was worth."

Drake rubbed his brow.

"What is it?" Sierra asked Drake—Colin and Alexandru were still speaking in Ukrainian.

"I just found out how the llama story ended," he said.

Sierra chuckled.

"Why are you here?" Alexandru asked. "Are you smuggling something? Is it these two guests? Do you need to hide something here? My rates have gone up, you know. The Romanian army aren't as easy to fool as they used to be. What with all that nonsense in Ukraine. The locals here are nervous. If Russia invades, this whole country will change—everything will change. I might not be able to help you anymore."

"It's always changing," Colin said. "When I first came here, you were a mechanic. Now, you're a farmer who moonlights as a smuggler's assistant."

"What's this about?" the farmer asked.

Colin knew he had to turn on the charm if he was going to convince Alexandru to help. He smiled, acted confident. "I have the business opportunity of a lifetime," he said.

Alexandru stirred the coffee and poured Drake, Colin and Sierra a cup. "What is it?"

"If you give me a vehicle, I'll give you fifty thousand euros," Colin said.

Alexandru placed the cups of coffee on the table and sat down. "When do I get the money?"

"Once I get back home," Colin said. "As soon as I get to Istanbul, I'll transfer you the money. The vehicle we're using—it won't get us across the border."

"Why not?"

"Do you watch the news?" Colin said.

Alxandru shook his head. "That's the red Toyota the whole Ukrainian military are looking for?"

Colin nodded.

"What the hell have you gotten yourself into?" the farmer asked.

"Trouble," Colin said. "But I think I can get out of it. I've got some help." He looked at his brother. "I think I'll be able to figure this all out. But I need your help. At the very least, you'll be fifty thousand euros richer. What do you say?"

"I'll help," Alexandru said. "You let me know that my marriage was a sham. You can take my Fiat 500."

Drake rolled his eyes. If there was one passion he had besides hockey, it was European vehicles. A Fiat 500 was a small vehicle. It resembled a Volkswagen Beetle and had a small engine. If that was the vehicle he and his brother were going to use to sneak into Turkey, he'd want another option. He grabbed Colin's wrist. "That's not good enough," he said in English.

"It's our only option," Colin said. "Let me go. Let me wrap up this deal."

Alexandru looked at Colin and Drake with skeptical eyes. "Is it a deal?"

"Yes," Colin said, responding to Alexandru. "We'll take the car. Thank you for the help."

Sierra looked at Drake and asked, "What's wrong?"

"The vehicle we're using is a clown car," he said. "If someone dangerous spots us—a cop or military vehicle—we'll be done for."

"Then I'll just have to get as far away from here as possible before they find me. I'll have to make sure that you have enough time to get to Turkey. I trust you, Jason. I know you can do this."

Drake looked at Sierra with a solemn expression. He knew she was finally beginning to understand what it was to be a CIA operative. She was willing to risk it all on an unsure plan.

Colin noticed the two of them looking at each other. "Are you ready?" he said to Drake. "We can leave now. This is our only option."

"We're ready," Drake said. "I'll get you to Istanbul."

"Thank you, brother."

FIFTY-THREE

After the conversation with Alexandru, Sierra got back inside the red Toyota and drove west from Cremshank toward Vienna—she'd never seen the city and heard it resembled Paris. She figured if she was captured, she might as well attempt to visit one of Europe's most beautiful cities. If she was going to spend months or years in a cell, she might as well make it worth her while.

Before leaving the sheep farm, Sierra and Drake spoke privately. "What do I do if I hear sirens?" she said.

"Pull over," Drake said. "You have to trust that me and Colin will be far enough away. You shouldn't risk your life over this."

"But I should risk my freedom?"

"Kate will do what she can do."

"She's only CIA Director for another day," Sierra said. "This is all happening at the wrong time."

"It always does."

"And what will you do once you get to Istanbul?"

"I'll send you and Kate everything I find out. As soon as we rescue Colin's wife, as soon as we make sure she's okay, I'll relay to you what he tells me."

"Do you trust him?"

"He's my brother."

"And if his information isn't valid?"

"Then we'll be back at square one," Drake said.

"And the Russian invasion of Ukraine? We could be held responsible if your brother is lying. We will have failed."

"We have to try," Drake said. "I'm sure there are parts of Colin's story that aren't true, but he is my brother."

Sierra kissed Drake as she stepped into the red truck would serve as a beacon of distraction. He kissed her back.

There was a connection between them. One built upon a foundation of loss and betrayal—one that he knew was genuine. They both had their reasons to hate the CIA: Drake for a drone strike that had killed children, Sierra for training a team of killers that murdered her mother. Yet, they had a bizarre and skeptical faith in Kate Price. Sierra was unlike so many others he'd met from the CIA. Her career only mattered to her insomuch as it helped her put a stop to bad people with bad aims.

Sierra looked at Drake in the rear-view mirror as she drove away from the farm.

She was careful not to attract too much attention to herself as she drove down the many roads out of Romania. She was sure to avoid major roads. She knew she had to be careful.

City through city, town through town, she didn't stop. She just kept driving. She did exactly what Drake had told her to do.

As she drove, she listened to local radio stations. While she didn't understand the native language, she was sure to listen for any phonetic sounds that resembled the truck's license plate.

As she crossed the border to the Czech Republic, she heard what sounded like her license plate from the news radio host.

They were on to her.

She'd been traveling for eight hours straight.

When she saw a pair of flashing red and blue lights in the mirror, she thought about trying to put on a chase. She thought about trying to evade capture, but she took Drake's advice.

She pulled over.

Her game was up. She just hoped Drake and Colin were far enough away.

FIFTY-FOUR

"Is this a CIA op?" Eli Chambers yelled. The National Security Advisor of the President was on the phone with Kate and the President. He was speaking so loudly, his voice distorted.

Price was in her office and kept hitting 'refresh' on her computer's web browser, hoping that some news brief would clear her of any involvement. She nervously scanned the headlines of various news outlets. So far, no one had tied the CIA to anything, but she knew it was only a matter of time.

"It's not CIA," she said.

"If this is a CIA operation, Kate," President Clarkson grumbled, "you do understand that I will have you arrested."

"The woman who was arrested outside of Prague was American," Eli said. "I've got a team running an identification on her right now. If we confirm that she is affiliated with the CIA, you understand the trouble you'll be in?"

"Then I'll await your team's assessment," Price said.

"Kate, I know you wanted us to get involved in this conflict," President Clarkson said. "I know you felt this was about stopping the next Cold War, but this is ridiculous. Eli knows more about Russia and Makarov than you. Why do you think I made him the NSA? He was our Russian ambassador for five years. He knows how Makarov thinks. If Makarov is going to make a move, then I know I can trust Eli to tell me the truth. He's been right about everything so far. And you ... well, let's just say your record doesn't help your cause."

Price kept hitting 'refresh'. As long as the Czechs hadn't yet pulled from Sierra that she was a CIA officer, she was in the clear. She, of course, knew that Sierra was the one who had been captured in Prague. She didn't have to look at the intercepted images or read the intercepted comms to know that it was her.

Still, she knew she had to play dumb, if only to give herself and Sierra more time.

She wanted to find out what the hell was going on. She wanted to find out why Sierra was in Prague. Wasn't she supposed to be in Kyiv?

As questions flooded her mind, the President spoke: "With Eli's help, I've sent a task force to Prague. Since the woman captured is American, at least based on released reports from the Czech intelligence services, I'm skeptical, Kate. I worry that you gave approval to an operation that may have put our chances of a peaceful resolution into jeopardy. You went against my orders."

"You should do what you feel you must," Price said.

"We will," Eli said.

The conversation ended shortly after.

Price was alone in her office. She had no one in Langley she felt she could trust. She worried that if she brought anyone else into the situation, they'd rat her out to Eli—the cretin had it out for her. He considered her a threat.

Instead, Price called the only person she trusted. The only man left in the world she trusted. She didn't want to have to call him, but she had no choice.

"What is it?" Colt said. "I told you not to call me on my work phone."

"How's London?" she asked. "You've been gone for a few days now. The house feels empty without you."

"The lads are alright. Typical training recruits. They're all soft."

"Good."

"What is it, love? What's going on?"

"Can you help me?"

"What's it about?"

"Russia, Ukraine—maybe world war."

"Isn't that what it's always about?" Colt said.

"Will you help?"

"Depends."

"Sierra White, my former assistant, now officer out in the field, has been apprehended by the Czech police. Can you get her out of there and back to DC?"

"If I don't?"

"I could end up in jail? Russia could invade Ukraine? A new Cold War? I don't know."

"It's one of those situations, is it?"

"Yes."

"Do you know what jail?"

"No."

"I'll figure it out, love. I'll get a team on it."

Price hung up and logged out of her computer. It was one of her last days at the office. She was about to give up an incredible amount of power and all because she couldn't play along with DC politics.

She left the office, left Langley, and drove home.

FIFTY-FIVE

The drive from Cremshank to Istanbul was uneventful. The sun set and rose—nature and time moved as they always did. Like clockwork, things unraveled.

Drake and Colin spent hours together in the Fiat 500—Drake's left shoulder brushed up against the left front window constantly. The vehicle was almost comically small—a clown car, he'd called it. It was an uncomfortable ride, to say the least.

"Are you sure you don't want me to drive, brother?" Colin asked, noticing Drake's discomfort.

"It's fine."

Colin asked the question many times over the ten-hour drive from Cremshank. But Drake didn't care about being uncomfortable. His mind was concerned with other matters.

He wanted to know the truth about Colin. So if he was happy about one thing, it was that the long drive gave the brothers time to talk.

"How did mother die?" Colin asked. It was the first time he'd mentioned their mother since Drake had pulled him out of Temny.

"Dave."

"Dave killed her?"

Drake nodded.

Hours passed before they spoke again. Mountains and coastal landscapes transformed into one another. They left Romania and began the drive through Bulgaria.

Colin broke the silence. "I'm sorry," he said.

"Sorry for what?" Drake grunted.

"Sorry for putting you through this."

"Through what?"

"Stop being an ass," Colin said. "You thought I was dead. You had no reason to suspect otherwise."

"Why did you fake your death?"

"I left home when I was young. I was a damn fool. A kid. I struggled for years. I worked for two-bit criminals—the kind that rob gas stations and cars in Walmart parking lots. I tried to survive. I knew if I was going to live on my own, I needed to find a job that paid well— and consistently."

"That's when you joined the military?"

"Yes," Colin said. "I went to a recruitment office. They didn't give a shit about my past. I was nineteen. They let me in. I went to Iraq—and I died."

"How did you die?"

"I was on patrol. We were walking the streets of Fallujah. Everything seemed normal, and then a bomb went off. It killed our squad leader. I fell to the ground, shrapnel embedded in my leg. If not for the help of some locals, I would have been dead."

"Why'd the military think you were dead?"

"Because I didn't go back to base, and they found fragments on my flesh in the dirt. I think they thought I'd been blown to smithereens," Colin said. "I stayed in Fallujah. I stayed in that Iraqi village. My legs were chewed up, muscle was turned to mush. I didn't join the army for some grand cause—I joined the military to leave Texas and make something of myself. All I wanted was a way out."

"So you stayed hidden? You pretended to be dead? You selfish asshole."

"Selfish? I was a kid. I didn't know what my actions would cause. I was just trying to do what I could to get by. I figured that if the army thought I was dead, I could disappear. Which is what I did. I moved to Istanbul, found some work—that's how I ended up working for the Company."

"And you you think that's okay?"

"I'm not saying it's okay," Colin said. "It's probably not. It's probably all messed up. I left you, and now—hearing that Mom died because of Dave—I'm sick. I made mistakes."

"I don't care about your past," Drake said. "I came to Kyiv because I wanted to put to rest my feelings that you could be alive. I figured that whoever was in the Ukrainian facility was just some asshole who'd heard my name from you while you were a soldier. I hoped that my brother wasn't some dickhead who lied and cheated his way through life."

Colin scoffed. "Did you not ever know me? All I was was an asshole. I lied and cheated through everything, brother. I wasn't the man you thought I was. I wasn't even yet a man when I disappeared from your life. I was a boy with a lost father."

"So was I."

The two of them crossed the border into Turkey and drove straight to Istanbul. As they pulled up to the Turkish capital, Drake heard the news over the radio about Sierra.

"The red Toyota truck that Ukrainian officials have been looking for has been found outside off Prague," the news reporter said.

"I think we're in the clear," Drake said as he drove toward downtown Istanbul. "Sierra has been captured. She sacrificed everything to protect us. She gave up her freedom. You'd better not be lying to me—you better tell me everything about the people who hired you."

Colin shrugged. "Take me home, and I will reveal everything."

FIFTY-SIX

A man stood at the doorway of Sierra's cell. The door to her cell was open. He was dressed in an expensive suit. A lawyer? Someone from the CIA? Sierra studied his silhouette. She tried to determine if he looked familiar. Was he someone she knew from Langley?

He wasn't.

The man at the door turned to the guards and handed them something—an envelope?

The man in the suit walked up to her and knelt down. He was close enough that she could now see his face. "Are you okay?" he asked in English. He had a thick Scottish accent.

It was Colt.

"What the hell?" she said.

"Keep calm, lassie," he said. "You did good. You got Jason far enough away to buy him time. I'm sure that was your ploy. But now we need to be cool. You need to play dumb and come with me. If you want to get back to America, you have no other choice. Do you understand?"

She nodded.

"Good girl," Colt said.

He took her by the hand. The two of them stood up. She was cold and felt weak—they'd hardly fed her since she got into the cell.

"Follow me," he said.

He guided her out of the holding cell and took her into a small room in the police facility. She sat on a chair, and listened to Colt and the Czech officials argue. After a long conversation, Colt handed them another envelope—it looked just like the one he'd handed the guard when he'd entered her cell.

They looked inside the envelope, looked at Sierra, and nodded at Colt.

Colt turned to her and helped her up from the plastic chair. He guided her out of the room.

"What's going on?" she said.

"I just convinced the Czech police that you weren't worth their time," Colt whispered.

"How?"

"I paid them ten thousand dollars. Although, they'll figure it out soon enough that you're worth far more. They think the red truck you were in isn't the same truck the Ukrainians were looking for."

"Won't they run the plates?"

"They just did," Colt said. "I paid these assholes twice to run the plates."

"Won't they find out I was driving the same truck they're looking for? Isn't this a waste of time?"

"I'm on an SAS mission, sweetheart. I've got a team just outside this facility making sure that whatever plates they run show up what I want to show them. At least, for the time being. As soon as we're off the premises, we'll be on the run. Keep your wits about you and play along. It might get messy. But if we get out of this police precinct, we'll get you home. I promise you that."

Sierra walked nervously alongside Colt. They left the precinct.

As Colt expected, the cops inside realized that they'd made a mistake.

The SAS officers inside the small white Mercedes van outside the precinct opened the doors. Colt and Sierra jumped inside.

They sped off.

They drove through Prague in a whirlwind. They drove until the authorities lost their trail. Once they were sure they were in the clear, they drove out of the city to a remote location.

A helicopter was waiting for them.

As Sierra got inside the helicopter, she asked Colt." Has anyone heard from Jason?"

"No," Colt said.

She smiled. No news was good news.

She watched the forest floor turn small as the helicopter rose into the air. It flew her to an RAF base in Germany. Once it landed, she discovered the truth about Drake.

It wasn't good.

FIFTY-SEVEN

Istanbul was cluttered with bumper-to-bumper traffic. The sound from honking cars was incessant. But the only thing Drake wished for was proper air conditioning—the Fiat 500's AC was busted. The only way to escape the heat was to open the windows, which made the whole car smell like fumes.

"Where is your house?" he said to his brother.

"It's just down this street," Colin said.

"Would it be easier on foot?"

Colin looked up and down the street. "It might."

"Then let's do it."

Drake stepped out of the vehicle and started to jog down the street. Colin did his best to keep up. The vehicle they'd got from Alexandru remained idle in the middle of the road.

"Hurry up," Drake yelled at Colin.

"You need to slow down. I don't have your endurance."

Drake stopped at a major intersection and waited for Colin to hobble to his side. Colin stopped running a couple of hundred meters earlier.

"You need to keep up," Drake said.

"You need to slow down," Colin said, panting and holding his chest. "It hurts to breathe. We're going too fast."

"You said your wife is in danger," Drake said. "If my wife was in danger, I wouldn't stop running."

"I'm doing my best."

Colin gave directions, and he and Drake ran the rest of the way.

The condo where Colin lived was located in the heart of the city. It was a thirty-story building and looked modern. It was like a glass obelisk in the middle of the ancient city. It stood out. Its lines were sharp, and its windows were broad.

At the entrance, Drake had to wait for Colin. His older brother couldn't keep up.

"Will the man at the desk know your face?" Drake asked.

"It's where I live. Of course, they know my face."

The two brothers walked into the building. The man who stood at the lobby's check-in nodded at Colin. Drake followed his brother toward the elevators.

A new thought struck his mind. He was about to see his brother for maybe the last time. After he helped Colin with his wife, he didn't know what Colin would do, but Drake had no reason to assume that he'd continue to be a part of his brother's life.

His brother would be dead to him. Again.

But not in the same sense.

In a way that felt more permanent.

As the elevator rose up to the fifteenth floor, Drake looked at his brother. The man he'd thought dead was resourceful, if weak. He was a man who, just a day earlier had accepted death. But still, he was a man who was willing to give it all up to protect his family. Drake knew he'd have done the same.

When the elevator doors opened, he followed Colin toward his apartment. He soon learned just how different the two brothers were.

FIFTY-EIGHT

Hours earlier

Artem arrived in Istanbul undetected. He left the stolen cop car at the edge of the city and took a cab to the inner core.

"Where you headed?" the cabbie asked.

Artem told him the address—the one given to him by the Company.

"Swanky neighborhood, eh? Another rich foreigner."

"Yes," Artem said. "I'm just another rich foreigner. I'll pay you double if you're quick."

"Sounds like a plan."

The cabbie sped through the dense streets and pulled to a stop outside a condo building.

Artem paid him and left the vehicle. He walked into the lobby and spoke to the concierge. "My business has a room rented on the fifteenth floor of this building."

"Whose name it is under?"

Artem told the man the name.

"I'll need to call," the concierge said.

"Of course."

Artem waited. The Company had rented the room a day earlier.

"May I see your ID?"

Artem handed the concierge his ID, the same one he'd picked up in Russia at the start of the mission.

"Here's your key, sir."

"Thank you."

Artem didn't go up to his room, however. Instead, he sat in the lobby.

He'd be waiting for them.

His target was coming.

There was no other reason for him to head to Istanbul.

FIFTY-NINE

Colin knocked on his door. A woman answered. Drake stood behind him in the hallway.

"You need to leave," Colin said to the woman.

"But, my love—"

"Leave!" he shouted.

"You've been gone for days—"

"Leave! Get out of here."

She could tell by the tone of his voice that he wasn't joking around. She left the condo. She scurried down the hallway, pushing past Drake

Drake walked up to his brother. "Was that your wife?"

Colin shook his head nervously. "She's my... cleaning lady."

"What? Where is your wife?"

"The men I work for know I live here. Do you think I would have her stay here?"

Drake grabbed his brother's shoulder. "What is this about, Colin? Tell me the truth."

Colin pulled free from Drake's grip and walked into his condo. Drake followed.

The place was nice. It had multiple floors and a grand vista view of Istanbul. Large floor-to-ceiling windows made it feel bright. It was decorated in a modern fashion. The furniture was clean and spare. The walls weren't cluttered with paintings or pictures. Instead, whatever was hung up was meant to exaggerate negative space.

Drake followed Colin to a room in the back of the apartment. "Where is your wife?"

Colin walked up to a computer and logged in. He turned back to his brother, who was standing at his office doorway. "About that, brother," he said.

Before Colin could type anymore, Drake grabbed his brother by the throat. "What the hell is this?" he said. "Are you married or not? Why are we here?"

"We're here for a reason," Colin said, his face turning blue. "Will you let me go?"

"Why should I let you go?"

"Because you're my brother?"

"Find a better reason!"

Colin laughed. "I'm an asshole," he said. "You should just kill me—"

"You idiot," Drake grunted. He released his grip on his brother's throat.

Colin turned back to his computer.

"What are you doing?" Drake said.

"Give me a second."

Drake pulled his brother back from the computer. He then saw what Colin was doing: Colin was deleting files. He was wiping the drive clean.

"What the hell?" Drake said.

"These files need to be deleted," Colin said. "It might be the only way I survive this. I need to delete everything that connected the Company to that deal in Ukraine. I think this is my way out. You could join, brother. We could do this together."

Drake went to hit cancel on the computer, but Colin jumped on his back and grabbed him by the neck. "Don't! This is the only way!"

"You had me drive you from Ukraine to Istanbul so we could delete some files. Do you even have a wife?" Drake tossed his brother off his back.

Colin fell to the floor. "I haven't been telling you the whole truth. There's more to this. There's information that I know you will want to know, but there's information that can't exist. When you pulled me out of that cell in Kyiv, I came up with this plan. I'll show them that I deleted everything. Maybe then, they'll let me live."

Drake hit cancel. But the files' deletion was partially complete. He scrolled through the computer's file system. He was looking for something, anything on Ukraine.

His brother was trying to delete a group of files called LOTUS. He opened up a random file and saw that it was a series of receipts and emails. Colin had kept tabs on everything.

Drake opened some more of the files. "How long have you been working for them?" he asked his brother.

"A long time," Colin said.

"Who are they?"

"They're an American company—but they work internationally. They pay well."

"Clearly."

"You need to delete those files," Colin said.

"If I don't?"

"I'm a dead man."

"You keep saying that," Drake said. "But you're still alive."

"They know I live here," Colin said. "We don't have much time. Once they've learned I'm still alive, I'm sure this will be the first place they come to."

"We're taking this computer to Langley. You're coming with me."

Colin remained silent.

Drake continued to scan through the documents. He was looking for a name or address.

"Colin?" Drake said, turning around.

Colin had picked up a small ornament from his bookshelf. He whacked Drake across the temple.

Drake fell to the ground, unconscious. "I'm sorry, brother. This is for your own good."

He dragged Drake into the corner of the room and walked back to his computer. He deleted everything. He made sure his entire hard drive was wiped clean.

Outside, thick, heavy clouds rolled over the condo. It made it look like the Colin's apartment was within a cloud.

He sat down at his desk, exhausted.

SIXTY

Artem saw the cleaning lady leave Colin's apartment. He'd followed Drake and Colin up from the lobby.

He pulled out his pistol and stopped her as she ran down the hallway. "Do you have a key to that room?"

The woman fell to her knees. Tears streamed from her eyes. She handed Artem the key.

"Good girl," Artem said.

He whacked her in the temple with his pistol. She fell to the floor.

He heard shouting from the two men he'd been following.

He walked cautiously into the condo and listened. He waited for them to stop and then walked up to the small room they were in. He lifted up his pistol.

One of the men was on the ground, unconscious. The other was at his computer.

He walked into the room and aimed the pistol at the man on the computer. His target. Colin Drake.

COLIN SAW Artem and raised his hands. "Everything is deleted," he said. "No one will have any idea that the Company is connected to me. That's why I came here."

"You were supposed to die in that facility," Artem said. "You know the drill. You know what you were supposed to do."

"I wanted to die. I wanted to have it all end there ..." He looked at his brother. "But then he got involved. None of this was supposed to happen. I didn't want to be rescued."

Artem walked into the small office, his pistol still aimed at Colin. "You think that by deleting those files, they'll let you live."

"I deleted everything: transcripts, addresses, receipts. No one will be able to trace any of this to the Company. They'll be clear."

"But it's what's in your head that is the problem."

"I won't say a thing. And, anyway, I'm out of the prison. They don't even know who I am. I'm a ghost. You need to let me walk. I'll go with you. I'll go to the headquarters."

Artem giggled. "You're stupid," he said. "What a stupid plan. Why on earth would they let you back?"

"Because I was a damned good smuggler?"

"You got yourself caught."

"Well maybe next time we shouldn't be dealing with two-bit Ukrainian rebels. Those assholes are the reason I was caught. They pretty much told everyone and their neighbor what they were picking up. I knew that it was a shit job. I should've turned it down."

"But you didn't."

"I was told to deliver goods to a group of rebels in Ukraine—I wasn't expecting them to be imbeciles."

"I'm done with this conversation."

"I'm surprised you wanted to talk in the first place."

"I wanted to thank you. Most of my kills have come too easy. You're the first challenge I've had in many years. It made me feel alive again. Now, close your eyes. Goodby—"

ARTEM WAS ABOUT to pull down on the trigger but was stopped after Drake, who'd pushed himself up from the floor, hit him in the back of the head with a small stone angel he'd grabbed from Colin's mantel. Artem fell to the ground, holding his head. The Russian assassin rolled on the ground.

Colin looked at Drake. His eyes wide with shock. "Thank you, brother. I'm sorry I attac—"

"Shut the fuck up! Just grab his gun," Drake said. His voice was slow, labored. He was still feeling the effects of Colin's attack. His steps were uneven. He wasn't fully conscious. He looked like he was about to fall over.

"Are you okay?" Colin asked.

"No," Drake grunted. "You asshole. You could have killed me. Just get him. Get his gun. He's still movi—"

Artem pushed himself up from the floor with an athletic grace. A wide smile spread across his face. With his left hand, he felt the back of his head—where Drake had hit him. He looked at his hand. It was covered in blood. "You're the reason this miscreant lived? You're the reason I've gone through all this trouble."

Drake shook his head and cracked his neck. He readied himself for combat. "Drop the weapon."

Artem aimed the pistol at Drake. His hand wobbled on account of the blow he'd taken. "Who are you? Why'd you save him?"

"Drop the gun," Drake growled.

Artem laughed. "Or what? Who are you? Why'd you save this asshole? You should have just let him die."

"Are you going to shoot me or not?" Drake said. He was beginning to feel better, less woozy. He spit on the ground between them. "Come on!"

Artem sighed. "I don't want to. After all this effort, this feels far too easy. But, I was sent here to kill ..." Artem looked around the office. During his brief exchange with Drake, he'd lost track of Colin. "Where the hell did he go?"

Drake had been keeping an eye on Colin. His brother knew how to survive. "He's gone," Drake said. "He left the office."

Artem shrugged. "Whatever," he said. "He won't go far once you're dead."

"What is Lotus?" Drake asked.

Artem paused. "Lotus? That idiot. He's told you far too much. It's best for people like yourself not to concern with—"

Colin hadn't left the room. Instead, he'd been hiding behind a small desk. He charged at Artem, tackling the assassin to the floor. Artem fired three shots. Drake dove to cover. Colin and Artem fought. The two men exchanged blows.

Drake slowly pushed himself up the floor. He shook his head.

Artem punched Colin in the kidneys and elbowed him in the head. As Colin was caught off guard by Artem's aggressiveness, violence. Artem was like a rabid animal—frenzy, bloodthirsty.

Artem grabbed hold of Colin's head and jabbed his thumbs into Colin's eyes. He pushed down. He could feel the eyeball compress deep into the socket. Colin wailed.

Drake, still weak and groggy, flung himself at Artem. He tackled the assassin and the two men rolled on the floor.

Colin moaned and held his hands to his eyes. He rolled back and forth on the floor.

Drake and Artem fought. It was bloody. Violent. Their brief melee lasted for no more than thirty seconds, but it was long enough. They'd met their equal. Their match. The two men stood across from each other in the small office.

Drake spit blood out onto Colin's expensive carpet. The Russian assassin had broken a rib and fractured his ankle. He knew it. The killer knew how to fight.

Artem stood across from Drake in a similar state. His left shoulder sunk on account of the elbow Drake had delivered to him and his jaw was clearly broken. Drake fought just as dirty as he did.

"You're going to lose," Artem said. "Just accept your fate."

Drake didn't respond. Instead, he just readied himself for more. He looked back at his brother, who was still on the floor.

Colin's eyes were closed, but blood was dripping from them. He had hands sprawled out on the floor. He was looking for the pistol that Artem had dropped.

Sensing the threat, Artem made his move. He charged at Drake. Kicking and counter punching when necessary.

Drake warded off the attacks when possible and bore the brunt of the pain when necessary. He was losing. He knew that the fist fight would be over soon.

COLIN KNEW his eyesight was gone. He was blind. When he tried to open his eyes he just felt pain. He saw nothing.

Everything he'd been running from was coming to close.

He was finally paying the price for the life he'd been living.

He deserved it.

But his brother didn't.

He couldn't let Drake die for his misdeeds.

He scrambled on his knees, his arms extended. He felt with his hands across his Persian carpet, the one he'd specially ordered from an arms dealer in Iran who hid his operation by selling expensive carpets. He needed to find the pistol. It was his only hope.

He could hear Drake's grunts and groans. He knew his brother losing.

He needed to find it.

He needed too ...

Finally.

ARTEM HELD Drake by the collar. He lifted up his fist and looked down at the bloodied mysterious man who'd caused him so much trouble.

"Who the fuck are you?" Artem asked. "What agency do you work for?"

Drake spit up some blood and smiled a toothy grin, albeit red-stained grin. "What do you care?"

"Just tell me! I want to know. I need to know. I need to know how you managed to evade my plans. You, sir, deserve a medal."

"Go fuck yourself."

"Typical American," Artem said. "Defiant till the end."

He was about to give the final deathblow when he saw Colin in his periphery. The blinded arms dealer was holding his dropped pistol. He had it aimed at Drake and Artem.

"No!" Artem hollered.

COLIN FIRED THREE TIMES. Artem rolled to cover. Drake fell to the floor, weakened to the point of almost death.

The shots exploded the wall-sized window at the far end of the office. A volley of wind rushed into the space.

Artem stood up. He walked up to Colin, who was still holding the gun but blindly turning left and right, unaware of Artem's location. Artem snatched the pistol from Colin and kicked the older and blind Drake brother in the head.

"That's it," he said. "Enough playing around. It's time to end this!"

"Ah, fuck you," Colin said. He was close enough to Artem to reach him with his feet. He swiped his legs in the direction of Artem's voice, causing the assassin to topple over.

Drake stood up, caught his breath, and lumbered over to the two men. He picked Artem up by the neck. He put him in a choke hold and walked backward to the opened window. Artem still had the gun in his hands. Drake was hoping the bastard would drop it to try to fend off his grip.

Instead, Artem completed his mission. He held the gun up while his face turned blue. He aimed it at Colin. He fired until the magazine was empty.

The bullets hit Colin in the stomach.

Drake howled with rage. With every ounce of strength left inside him he lifted Artem up and tried to toss him out the window. But the wily Artem took hold of Drake's neck as he was flung in the air.

The two men fell out of the window.

Drake twisted his arm back and grabbed the window's ledge.

Artem fell into the fog and disappeared.

Three fingers held Drake to the edge. He was badly beaten up and felt like shit.

He thought about letting go, but then he heard Colin's voice.

"Jas ... Jason ... I ..."

SIXTY-ONE

Drake clung to the outer edge of his brother's office window with his left hand. He could feel his fingers slipping. He swung his right hand up and got a better grip. Tiny fragments of glass that were still in the frame dug into his skin. He pushed past the pain and pulled himself up.

Colin was on the floor, doubled over. Blood pooled around him. Drake ran to his side. "Colin!" he shouted.

Colin spit up some blood. "I'm sorry," he said. "I'm sorry about everything."

"Shut up," Drake said. "I'll get you to the hospital. Hold on."

"Don't be stupid."

Drake looked at his brother's wounds. The bullet holes that had been dug into his stomach were spread out in a fashion that almost certainly meant he'd be dead in minutes, if not seconds.

Colin winced in pain—he couldn't move.

"Just try to hold on," Drake said, although he knew his request was in vain.

"I'm glad you tried to save me," Colin said, before coughing up more blood. "I'm glad we got to spend another couple of days together. You turned out alright. I was always a fool. I was more like Mom. You were more like Dad. You know, I think that's why I ran away. I realized that I wasn't like our old man. I wasn't ever going to live up to his memory..." he closed his eyes.

"Save your strength," Drake said. "I'll call for help. We'll get you out of here."

"You still think you can save me?" Colin said wearily. "You really are something, you know that? Despite everything, you want to help me. I betrayed you. I brought you here in a last-ditch attempt to save my ass. I was going to knock you out and disappear. I just didn't think that the assassin would be so close. I thought I had more time."

"Stop with this shit," Drake said. "Just shut up."

Colin eye's opened and closed—the pain was now too much for him to bear or even feel. "I can feel everything coming to the surface. There's no getting out of this. I'm done for."

Drake stood up and walked to the phone in Colin's office. He dialed the number of the concierge and ordered an ambulance.

Colin chuckled.

After the call, Drake rejoined his brother. He tried to compress the wounds—stop the bleeding. He didn't care that it was hopeless. He had to try.

"The Company is big," Colin said, his voice almost a whisper or a gurgled mess of blood and noise.

"What company?"

"Lotus. The men who hired me," Colin said. "They're based in Washington. They're operated by a guy high up. Rumor has it the Russians have *kompromat*, compromised information on the fucker. He was a diplomat to Russia for a few years, I think."

"What are you saying?"

"I'm telling you everything," Colin said. His eyes seemed to fade more with each breath. "I'm making things right. Maybe you can correct my wrongs—that seems to be your expertise."

Drake stared into his brother's eyes. Colin was finally living up to his memory of him.

"I was hired to deliver chemical weapons to the Crimean rebels so they would use them on Russian soldiers. The goal was to start a war, I think. The mission was simple: deliver the goods and leave. But it was clear what they were doing. I was given the mission because I was the best. Like I said, rumor has it the Company, Lotus, was working for the Russian President. The Russians wanted a reason to invade Ukraine."

Colin couldn't speak anymore; the pain was too much.

"Keep your strength," Drake said.

Colin wiped his mouth. "I've got no reason to keep fighting," he said. "I know you'll shut them down. I've been running my whole life, and I know you'll make it right. You'll end Lotus. You'll end the Company."

Colin's eyes closed. He stopped breathing.

Drake held him until emergency services personnel rushed into the room. They tried to resuscitate his brother. They failed. Still, he joined them in the ambulance.

He made a call—one that he didn't want to make, but one that he had to.

PART THREE - VENGEANCE

SIXTY-TWO

Sierra ran through the hallways of the hospital in Istanbul. With the help of the SAS, she got to the city in no time. Drake had reached out to Price—but he said he had important information. Information that could change everything.

He was in the hospital lobby.

"Jason," she said. "Are you okay?"

He embraced her.

"I'm fine," he said.

"I heard about Colin. I'm sorry."

"I know who he was working for."

Above the soda machine in the lobby, hung up on the wall, was a television. It showed a constant stream of news.

"Who is it?" Sierra asked.

"Some organization called Lotus. The man who runs the operation is high up in DC. He was a Russian diplomat."

A man appeared on the television. It was National Security Advisor. Eli Chambers. He was about to give a press conference about the situation in Ukraine. Apparently, Russian forces were pulling back from the border.

"Oh my god," Sierra said. "Are you sure?"

"That's what Colin said."

Sierra looked up at the television. "That's Eli Chambers. He's an ex-Russian diplomat. He's the President's right-hand man and the reason why Kate's been fired."

"You need to tell Kate that he is our target," Drake said.

Both Drake and Sierra watched Eli's conference.

"We are happy to hear that the attack in Kyiv didn't further escalate the conflict between Ukraine and Russia," Eli said. "We're satisfied President Makarov will find a peaceful resolution. But if Russia feels the need to defend itself, I am confident that President Clarkson will do the right thing. He won't get involved. He'll keep us out of it. He'll stay far away. It's the right thing for the President to do."

Sierra looked at Drake, "What do you mean?"

"Eli runs Lotus," Drake said.

"Are you sure?"

"My brother died telling me the truth."

"You sure he didn't lie?"

"Yes."

"Who killed him? Who attacked you?"

"The assassin who tried to kill us in the Temny Facility, I think. I don't know for sure. The bastard was good. He almost killed me."

"And what happened to him?"

"I pushed him out the window of my brother's fifteenth-floor condo apartment. He should be dead."

Sierra hugged Drake. "We need to head to Washington. You need to tell this to Kate."

Generally, Drake would have resisted the call to go to Langley, but he knew he had to go. He had to make sure that Price followed through with the information he was about to give her. He wasn't about to let his brother's death mean nothing.

He had to make Eli Chambers pay.

SIXTY-THREE

It was the last day of Price's role as CIA Director. She relayed to the President the information Sierra had sent her—the information from Drake.

President Clarkson wanted to speak to her, one on one. The two of them were in the oval office. It was a cloudy and cool day. Clarkson had the window open. It looked like it was going to rain.

"Are you sure this is accurate?" Clarkson said.

"I'm positive."

"How?"

"It comes from Jason Drake. The man who saved your life."

"He was also the man accused of killing me."

"Don't be stupid. You need to give me authorization to raid Eli's offices. We can get to the bottom of this."

"You're no longer CIA director," Clarkson said.

"What does that mean?"

"I think you know what that means."

"Come on, Roy. You know he's an asshole. Jason believes that Makarov has compromising materials of Eli. This could go right to the Russian President."

"You really think the Russian President would attack his own troops? Do you hear yourself? You want me to believe that the President of Russia hired some smuggler to deliver chemical weapons to Ukrainian rebels to stage an attack against Russian troops? All in an effort to justify a war."

"Yes, I do," Price said. "And Eli was using his political sway over you to keep out of the conflict."

"So, you think I'm some useful idiot?"

"I think you're a man trying to maintain control in a world that is clearly out of control ... sir."

"Get out of my office," Clarkson said. "You're wasting my time."

Price smiled. "So, that's how you want to end things?"

"End things?" Clarkson said. "You're nuts, Kate. I should have never trusted you. Hell, it was your men who put a bullet in my neck. You're done at the CIA and I am done with you. President Makarov wants peace. You said he'd invade, and he didn't."

"He pulled back because Jason interfered."

"And where is Jason right now? I should have him arrested, you know! He shouldn't have been interfering with international relations. He could have sparked a war."

"He stopped one."

"Oh please," Clarkson said. He picked up his phone. "Can you have the secret service escort ex-CIA Director Kate Price out of my office? Thank you." He hung up.

"You've changed," Price said.

"I've grown smart," Clarkson said. "I've realized that trusting you was my biggest mistake."

Two secret service members walked into the oval office. Price rolled her eyes and stood up. "So, you're just going to deny the information I shared with you? You're going to keep Eli Chambers as your NSA?"

"Yes."

"So be it," Price said. She thanked the President and left the White House. She made her way back home. Usually, the President was her most important meeting of the day, but not today.

SIXTY-FOUR

Drake waited for Price. He'd come back to DC with Sierra. During the flight from Istanbul, Price acted on the intel Drake had been told by his brother.

After they stepped out of the aircraft, Sierra turned to Drake. "She wants to speak with you."

"About what?"

"I don't know," Sierra said. "All I do know is, she isn't happy."

Drake shook his head.

A CIA SUV drove him to Price's house. The man at the door told him she was meeting with the President. He told Drake to wait in the study.

She arrived thirty minutes later.

"Jason," Price said. "What a surprise." She didn't look surprised.

"I hoped this day would never come," he said.

Price mockingly laughed. She sat down. "Thank you for the information. You... didn't save the day."

Drake's eyebrow rose. "What do you mean?"

"The intel about the Lotus organization and Eli Chambers ..." She drifted off and looked out her window. "President Clarkson didn't buy it. He refused to believe anything I told him."

"He's an idiot," Drake grunted.

"Well, do you have any proof?"

"No," Drake said. "Every bit of intel I had was destroyed."

"How?"

"My brother deleted it from his hard drive."

"I'm sorry about your brother."

Drake shrugged. "It doesn't matter."

The two of them stared at each other in silence. They didn't know what to say. The world felt like it was collapsing around them, but they both felt something else, too. A sensation that they hadn't felt in a long time.

"Why did you agree to meet with me?" Price asked, breaking the silence.

"Sierra said you wanted to know what happened."

"You could have told me over the phone or simply had her relay it."

"I figured you wanted to hear it from the horse's mouth."

"Don't be silly, Jason. Why did you want to meet with me?"

He clenched his jaw and lowered his gaze. "How did you know I was alive? Every one in the Gerdansk facility was killed."

"I examined the death records. No one fit your description. If they would have found a tall, broad, blue eyed man—the Russians would have noted it."

Drake shook his head. "Are we done then?"

"Done? You've just started, Jason."

"Uh, no," he said. "I'm out. You're no longer CIA Director, either. There's nothing you have that can keep me around. I need to head back to Ruby—I need to check on Houston."

Drake stood up.

"Sit down," Price said. Her voice sounded authoritative, domineering—angry almost. It was a tone Drake hadn't heard much from Price. He looked at her defiantly.

"You have nothing to hold me back," Drake said. "I've given you everything I have so far. If you can't accept that, that's your problem."

"The woman in Syria ... what was her name?"

"Aya."

"Yes," Price said. "That woman. She was the woman who tried to attack the capital. She was the woman who brought you back to me after all those years."

"What about her?"

"In Gerdansk ... in the facility. After you saved us. We found someone. Someone you would want to know."

"What are you talking about? Get to the point!" Drake's voice grew loud.

"Aya had a daughter—"

"She died," Drake said cutting her off.

"No," Price said. "She didn't."

"Fuck you."

"There's the Jason Drake I know. Defiant. Angry. Stubborn. A man who despises the world. That's the man I recruited all those years ago. The young soldier who had no family."

Drake looked at Price and clenched his fists. "And you sound like the woman that recruited me. Sad and desperate. Trying to control an uncontrollable world ... and not caring how many people you piss off."

"Aya had a daughter, Jason. A daughter who is still alive. A daughter that I have protected. I can tell you where she is. She has your eyes, you know."

"Tell me where she is."

"Help me shut down Chambers."

"Where is she!?"

The front door to Price's house opened. Colt walked inside, holding a bag of luggage. He looked at Drake and Price in the living room and knew that something was wrong. "Everything okay, love?" he asked.

"It's fine," Price said.

Colt looked at Drake. "How are you, Jason?"

Drake seethed. He felt pierced in the heart. Unsure of what the news Price had just told him meant and questioning whether he could trust her or not. A daughter? A part of him wondered whether he should threaten Price to learn more, a part of him thought about accepting her mission to kill Chambers—the man responsible for his brother's fall.

"You okay, mate?" Colt asked.

Drake looked at the Scot and nodded. "I'm fine."

"If you help me bring Eli down, I will tell you where she is. I guarantee you that she is safe."

"Who are you talking about?" Colt asked, trying to catch up, trying to make sense of the tension.

"My daughter," Drake said.

"Daughter? Shite ... You told him. What's going on, love? What's this about?"

Price shot Colt a look that told him to shut up. "The Russian President has influence on the American President and Jason is going to help us bring it down."

"I thought you were done with the CIA," Colt asked.

"I am," she said.

"I'll help," Drake grunted. "I'll help and you'll tell me where she is. But if you think I'll ever forgive for you holding this against me, then you are mistaken. Our relationship is over. Once I shut down Eli Chambers, you tell me where she is and that's it. You understand?"

Price nodded. "Yes."

"Good." He left the living room and pushed past Colt, who gave him a worried look.

Drake walked out to the street and hailed for a cab. He needed to check-in to a hotel. He was going to be in DC longer than he wanted to be.

BUY BOOK FOUR - AVAILABLE NOW

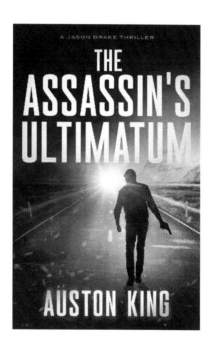

BUY NOW

ACKNOWLEDGMENTS

There were a series of people who helped make this book possible.
In order of no importance:
Meghan
Leighton
Jack
Lawrence
Denise
Karen
Steve
Dave
Sherrie
Linda
Frank
Thank you.

ABOUT THE AUTHOR

Auston King is an author based in the United States. The Assassin's Vengeance is his third full-length thriller. He lives with his wife, Meghan, his daughter, Leighton, and their pet chihuahua, Mya.

If you would like to reach out to Auston, please feel free to email him at austonking@creatorcontact.com or visit his Facebook page.

f

Made in United States
Orlando, FL
30 March 2023